WHAT DID ALL THESE
PEOPLE HAVE IN COMMON?

A gorgeous, swinging actress.
A super-straight married couple.
Two gay roommates.
A suburban housewife.
A black-and-white pair of business partners.
The answer was easy: Kate Arnheim.
But the hard-core truth that had turned one of
them from a tender lover into a savage mur-
derer was hidden far below the surface—
as Hardy probed intimate depths, felt out
sensual secrets, and moved toward a killing
climax. . . .

Books by Martin Meyers

Patrick Hardy Mysteries

Kiss and Kill
Spy and Die
Red is for Murder
Hung Up to Die
Reunion for Death

Dutchman Historical Mysteries
by Annette Meyers and Martin Meyers,
Writing as Maan Meyers

The Kingsbridge Plot
The High Constable
The House on Mulberry Street
The Lucifer Contract
The Organ Grinder
The Dutchman
The Dutchman's Dilemma

HARDY

RED IS FOR MURDER

Martin Meyers

SPEAKING VOLUMES, LLC
NAPLES, FLORIDA
2016

RED IS FOR MURDER

ISBN 978-1-62815-361-3

Chapter One

Patrick Hardy dialed Kate Arnheim's number and waited. Impatiently he hung up and dialed again.

"Hello," she answered breathlessly.

"Kate? It's me, Pat."

"Hi! Hold on a minute. I heard the phone ringing while I was still on the staircase. . . . How do you feel?"

"Great. That's why I called. They're letting me out today. Is our date still on?"

"You bet. And it starts as soon as you get here, so hurry up."

He hung up and smiled as he maneuvered his stiff left leg from the bed to the floor. When he started to shift his weight, he realized he had done it all wrong. He brought the left leg back up to the bed and swiveled around and put his right foot down first. Then he took the crutches from their position against the wall and stood up. He had been dressed and ready to go ever since Dr. Nesor had told him he could.

Dr. Nesor was the surgeon Dr. Merle Doyle had

sent Hardy to when his bad knee started giving more trouble than usual.

Now with a brand new scalpel scar next to an old bullet scar and minus some meniscus cartilage from his left knee, he was as happy to be leaving the hospital as he had been unhappy to be entering it four weeks before.

Charlie, the orderly, brought him a wheelchair.

"Who the hell needs that?"

"Sorry, Mr. Hardy, hospital policy."

"I'm touched by their thoughtfulness."

"It's not that," said Charlie. "They don't want anything to happen to you in the hospital . . . too many people suing them that way."

"My faith in humanity is restored," he said to Charlie, as the orderly trundled him to the cashier's office.

Outside on the street Charlie thanked him for the tip and left Hardy by the cab stand. The disabled detective shivered. It had been a mild autumn day when he had gone in. He tried to ignore December's promise of another New York winter and flagged a cab with his crutch. It worked. While the cab pulled up, he adjusted the flight bag straps on his shoulder.

After figuring out how to get into the cab, he did. Once inside he gave the driver Kate Arnheim's address in the west Eighties. They were at the brownstone in less than twenty minutes.

His first try at climbing stairs made him grateful that Kate lived only on the second floor.

"Oh, Pat. Look how pale you are!"

"Then how about getting me something for it, like some scotch."

"Sure. Coming up." She indicated the flight bag. "Is that your luggage?"

"Yeah, I'm traveling light."

"Well, don't just stand there, limp on in."

Kate established him on the couch with a drink, a cigarette, a lot of pillows, and herself.

She sipped his drink and took a drag of his cigarette. "What do you want to do first?"

"What are my choices?" he said as he moved his finger over the erect nipple that pushed against the fabric of her jersey dress.

"Well," she said, shivering in reaction, "I could feed you, or . . ."

"I'll take the second choice. They fed me in the hospital."

"How do we work it?" she asked.

"First you help me out of these pants, then we'll figure something out."

When he was down to his underwear, he picked up his crutches and made his way into the bedroom.

"Jesus. Your leg looks like it was in a concentration camp."

"Don't worry about it," said Hardy. "The bandage is just so I'll keep my knee straight. It's not even a cast."

"I wasn't talking about the knee . . . your thigh is skin and bone."

"Atrophied. Dr. Nesor told me it would happen. A couple of months of working out and it'll be fine."

"But what about now?"

"Get out of that dumb dress, and I'll show you."

He knew she had nothing on under her dress, and he watched in anticipation as she reached down to remove it.

Kate's figure was almost the ultimate of Hardy's fantasies. Long, thin, shapely legs, an almost boyish rear end and large breasts that didn't sag.

7

Slowly the dress rose. Those lovely legs. The black pubic patch. Her belly, glistening now with sweat. Those yearned-for breasts. All the weeks in the hospital he had thought of those breasts and the brown taut nipples.

The dress was off. She moved her long dark hair away from her face and knelt at the foot of the bed. Her lips were red and hungry.

Hands. Mouth. Tongue. Breasts. Their touch. Touching. Feeling. Being. Exploding.

Again. His fingers explored the wonder of her. Her tongue darted out as his hand touched her mouth. Along her chin and throat to that marvelous area between her two breasts . . . and then to that other marvelous area.

"Not your hands. You. I want you."

He was aware that she was talking.

"Nice. It's so nice. Oh, don't stop. You don't like to talk while you're doing it, do you? I do. I think it's nice. I think it's nice to talk about doing it while I do it. Now. Now. Now. Now!"

They came back from their sexually euphoric cloud and lit the obligatory cigarettes.

He kissed the breast closest to him. "How would you like to get up and get me a glass of water."

"Yes, sir."

"Sir? I thought you were a liberated woman!" Watching her ass as she padded off to get his water gave him new horny thoughts.

She was back with the water. She took a sip and passed it from her mouth to his. "I *am* liberated, on ordinary occasions, but you are not an ordinary occasion. You are pretty good stuff for a man with a stiff leg. I think there's a joke there somewhere. . . . You

8

know, what with your leg and all, I thought I'd have to be on top."

"That's not a bad way either," and he put aside the glass and caressed her belly.

"Forget it, wild man, I'm worn out . . . no. I mean it Pat, I'm not in the mood. I can't get turned on that fast."

"Are you sure?"

"Yes."

"Positive?"

"Pat . . . you persistent bastard. Oh, that's nice. That's very nice. Now do I get to ride on top?"

Sighs became moans and moans became screams and then sighs again as the tidal wave subsided. She snuggled close to him. "Did you ever see that movie with Gary Cooper on television?"

Patrick Hardy smiled. "You mean *For Whom the Bell Tolls?*"

"How did you know that was the one I meant?"

"Because, Katie, you beautiful-breasted marvelous piece, the earth moved for me, too. Now while I hobble to the toilet, why don't you get me something to eat, I'm starved."

Salad, steaks and baked potatoes and rosé and *Random Harvest* on television rounded out the rest of their evening.

In the morning they made love again and arranged for her to come to his place for Christmas eve dinner. Then she went to work and he went home.

Home was 7 Riverside Drive. Hardy crutched his way over to the Drive and downtown to the Seventies.

He undid all the locks to his street-level apartment. Inside he neutralized the alarm system and flopped down on the brown and black velvet chaise in his office and luxuriated in the joy of being home. After

9

several minutes of semi-dozing, he got up and shucked the flight bag from his shoulder and managed to get to the swivel chair at his desk. He called Laura, his housekeeper, to tell her he was home. He called his answering service and told them the same thing. They had some messages for him, but none of any consequence.

Several hours later Laura showed up followed by a delivery boy with lots of groceries and preceded by Sherlock Holmes, Hardy's black standard poodle.

"Ow," said Hardy as the dog's affectionate leap caused him to put weight on the bad leg. "All right, Holmes. That's enough. I missed you, too, now down. Down. That's better. Hello, Laura, how've you been?"

"The good Lord takes care of me. How are you, Mr. Hardy?"

"As well as can be expected. Thanks for looking after Holmes for me. I won't . . . ."

"Excuse me, Mr. Hardy," said Laura and went out to the kitchen to show the delivery boy where to put things and to let him out.

While the dog ran around sniffing the apartment, Hardy settled himself into the barber chair in his office and leaned back. He was tired. Holmes was now under his right hand demanding to be scratched.

"Mr. Hardy?"

"Yes, Laura?"

"Do you want me to make you something to eat?"

"No thanks, Laura. The sooner I start doing those things for myself, the better off I'll be. You can go now. I'll see you next week."

"No you won't. Next week is Christmas."

"That's right. I'll see you the week after . . . wait a minute." He hopped to his desk and wrote out a check to cover her salary and her Christmas bonus and a little more, and gave it to her. "Merry Christmas, Laura."

"Merry Christmas to you, too, Mr. Hardy, take care of yourself. Goodbye, Holmes."

The dog barked her out.

"All right. Okay. That's enough."

The happy poodle quieted down and came back for more ear scratching.

Hardy enjoyed the calm and silence for a while and then got some salami for himself and a dog bisquit for Holmes. While he munched he dropped notes to his two closest friends. Steve Macker, the sometime actor, was in Los Angeles and Ruby, the woman who set Hardy going just by thinking about her, was touring the Caribbean.

He thought about the first time he had seen Ruby's act. She had done a striptease to the music of *Swan Lake*. First she was dressed in a ballet costume. Then she was undressed, her red hair flowing and her body moving all over the place. He pushed the memory of Ruby's fantastic body in that purple light and later in bed, out of his mind.

He considered calling Kate Arnheim up and asking her to come over to his place after work. He rejected the thought. What he needed for the immediate future was rest and solitude.

The phone rang. It was a man who needed a detective to follow his wife. Grateful that he had to, Hardy refused the job and explained that he wasn't taking any cases for a while.

It rang again as soon as he hung up. This time it was the realty company that owned the building Hardy lived in. What with the operation and everything, he had forgotten to send in his rent check.

"Okay, honey, you tell Mr. Bunsen the check is in the mail. You can also tell him now would be a good time to make sure all the boilers are in working order so we all won't nearly freeze to death like we did last winter." He hung up without waiting for the woman to reply. It annoyed him that he had taken his pain and discomfort and his dislike for Bunsen out on someone who was just doing her job. He shrugged and went to the refrigerator for more salami and a bottle of ginger ale. He finished eating, washed down a vitamin E capsule, belched contentedly and lit a Marlboro. Hardy surveyed his bookcase. *Alice's Adventues in Wonderland & Through the Looking Glass.* He took it down. This time he chose the chaise, where Holmes joined him. He fell asleep just as the Caterpillar was telling Alice about Father William.

When Hardy awoke it was dark. He turned on the TV and went into the kitchen. He organized everything he needed on the French butcher table and propped himself against a stool to mix up garlic, paprika, flour and oil. He was supposed to stay away from salt because of his high blood pressure, but his taste sense won out over his common sense, and he added it to the mixture.

Hardy rubbed this into a three-pound chicken and put it into the oven to roast for an hour and a half at 375 degrees. He took some ground chuck out of the freezer for Holmes and went back to his book.

Besides working out in the gym next to his bedroom, he spent the next week in pretty much the same solitary manner. He didn't call Kate, and she didn't call him. They were going to spend Christmas Eve together, and whatever either of them did when they weren't seeing each other wasn't each other's business.

Chapter Two

Christmas Eve. The music and the hucksters on the radio had proclaimed it all day long. Hardy had watched parts of two different versions of *A Christmas Carol* on television. It was snowing.

He was getting along on one crutch in the apartment and no longer needed as much sleep as he had the first few days he was home.

The wine was chilling, the squabs were stuffed with wild rice and ready. The *creme genoise* was made. The table was set. The bed was waiting for them.

With all the work done, he shaved and then, after wrapping his leg with a towel and plastic food wrap, he took a hot shower.

Seven o'clock. Seven fifteen. At seven thirty he called Kate's number. No answer. At eight he called again. No answer. He wolfed down a cheese sandwich and called again at eight fifteen.

He was angry and disappointed. By nine thirty he had finished the wine and had called over a dozen times. He would call once more. He would wait till ten o'clock and then call just once more.

At five after ten Hardy dialed Kate's number. Twenty rings. Five more rings and he would hang up.

"Somebody help me . . ."

"Katie, it's me, Pat. What's wrong?"

"Dear Jesus, somebody please . . ."

"Kate! What's wrong, Kate? What's wrong?"

The line was still open, but she didn't answer.

Hardy hammered at the phone cradle with his finter to break the connection. He couldn't get an open line. He stopped and shouted, "Hold on, Kate," and depressed the receiver again and again until he got a line and was able to dial 911.

When the officer came on, Hardy told him what had happened and gave him Kate's address and apartment number. "Hurry, she sounds bad. I'll grab a cab and meet you there."

"What's your name please?"

"For Christ's . . . my name is Patrick Hardy. Hurry."

He shoved his keys and some money into his pocket and decided it would take too long for him to struggle into a coat. He grabbed his crutches and hurried outside. It was still snowing, and there were no taxis to be seen. Hopeful that ice hadn't formed beneath the snow, Hardy started the uphill trudge to Broadway.

Through some miracle he didn't slip, and through another, there was a cab letting people out just as he got to the corner.

He crawled in and gave the driver Kate's address. "You wouldn't have a cigarette?"

"Sure thing, buddy. Hey, your hands are shaking something awful. Maybe you need a drink."

14

"Never mind. Please, just hurry."

"Sure, I hurry, then I skid, and we're both dead. Relax, it's Christmas."

"Yeah. Yeah. Yeah," said Hardy and puffed on the cigarette.

When the cab pulled up to the brownstone, the squad car was already there, and two officers were out on the street looking up at the building.

Hardy worked his way to the sidewalk, talking as he moved. "I'm the one who called. Upstairs, second floor, rear. Hurry."

The older cop asked, "What seems to be the trouble?"

"I don't know. I was talking to her on the phone. She needs help."

"Well, what did she say?"

He was frantic. "Get upstairs, will you? I'll be right behind you."

"Hey, give me my money so I can get out of here. It's Christmas Eve."

Hardy leaned against a parked car and pulled some bills out of his pocket. He shoved them at the cab-driver and started after the policemen.

When he got to the second floor, the two men were in front of Kate's door. The younger one knocked. "Anybody home?"

"I tell you, she's in trouble," said Hardy. "Break down the door."

The older cop made a face. "And who pays for it if you're wrong?"

"Goddamn it, I'll pay for it. Open that fucking door."

"Take it easy, mister. You don't have a key?"

"No, I don't have a key. The owner lives on the first floor. Maybe he has one."

15

"Now we're thinking," said the older cop. "Jim, go down to the first floor and see if you can get the key."

"Sure thing, Max."

Handy started banging on the door. "Katie. Katie. It's me, Pat. Katie."

In a few moments Jim was back. "Nobody home."

"Okay," said Max, "get the stuff from the trunk. We'll pull the lock."

Hardy hammered and called Kate's name for what felt like an eternity until Jim came back upstairs with a large pair of pincers. He couldn't believe as he watched the two men apply the tool to the lock cylinder that they had ever used it before. They couldn't get any purchase on the cylinder. It kept slipping off.

"Will you please hurry."

"Do me a favor, mister," said Max, "shut up. We're doing the best we can.

While he sweated and watched, a part of Hardy's mind worked on the fact that despite all the commotion they were making, not one head had poked out of one door. Not one neighbor had looked to see what was happening.

The door was open. The kitchen light was on. Hardy started to go inside, but Max stopped him. "You were talking to her on the phone. Where would that be?"

"In the bedroom. To the right and right again."

Hardy's eyes focused on the Klee poster hanging on the kitchen wall. He thought about the other one in the bathroom where he and Kate had taken showers together.

Jim went by and into the hall. Max was in front of Hardy. "What did you say your name was?"

"Hardy. Patrick Hardy."

16

"Could you come into the bedroom please, Mr. Hardy . . . you better brace yourself."

There was blood on the floor. There was blood on the phone and on a batch of Christmas cards on the night table. The bed was soaked in blood. And Kate's once beautiful body lay in the bed, all mangled and red.

Hardy closed his eyes to blot it all out. He prayed for a miracle. But there were no Christmas miracles for Kate Arnheim. Kate Arnheim was dead.

Chapter Three

Hardy sat on the couch in Kate's living room while a small army of policemen attended to their particular duties.

He watched them and thought bitterly, Where were you when she needed you? His mind started imagining the unknown killer slashing at Kate with his knife. He didn't want to think about it, but he did think about it.

Different people asked him the same questions. Hardy answered them and waited until others asked the questions again. He had lost all track of time when an officer came over to him. "It's all right for you to go now, Mr. Hardy. My boss says I should drive you home."

Hardy nodded and they went.

He was grateful that the policeman didn't say anything along the way. Hardy thanked him and entered his apartment.

He looked around at what he had prepared for a Christmas Eve that never was and never would be.

Pouring himself a glass of Cutty Sark, he used it to wash down two tranquilizers then turned on the TV and started to undress. One of the versions of *A Christmas Carol* was ending and little Tiny Tim was asking God to bless everyone. He snapped off the set and turned on the radio. He dropped his jacket and shirt and tie to the floor and lay down on the chaise. Holmes came into the room yawning and stretching. He sniffed at Hardy's drink. Hardy put his finger in the scotch and let the dog lick it off. "Goddamn lush."

Holmes jumped up on the chaise and licked his master's face. "Lie down."

The animal did as he was told. Hardy lay there drinking and petting his dog and listening to Christmas music until the tranquilizers and the whiskey took effect.

He awoke rested. For several seconds he luxuriated in the warm corners of the chaise and the peaceful corners of his mind. Then in one quick flash reality rushed back to him. Hardy tried to banish it, but the fact of Kate Arnheim's death would not go away.

He looked at his watch. It was just after ten. He felt he should do something . . . what? He went to his desk and started to dial a number. Midway he stopped and hung up. He went into the kitchen and poured himself a glass of orange juice and sipped it slowly while he stood by the window and watched the morning sun shining on the still white snow.

What?

He shaved and washed and ate breakfast and stared out at the snow, which was now more gray than white.

Hardy started to think about Kate. The feel of her body, the taste of her. He broke his reverie with a false laugh when he realized that he was on the way to convincing himself that he had been in love with Kate. Not so. But still he thought he should do something.

Back to his desk and his phone. When he was connected with Manhattan North, he asked for Detective Gerald Friday.

"What is it, Private Detective?" said the cop derisively.

"I need a favor."

"To repeat what you said to me recently, since when are we on favor terms?"

It crossed Hardy's mind to hang up. Instead, "When I need a favor and someone can give me one, then I'm on favor terms with him."

Friday was enjoying this. "What about the other way around?"

"All right," said Hardy, "you've made your point. I'll owe you."

"As long as you put it that way, what can I do for you?"

"You should be seeing a report from Homicide pretty soon about a Kate Arnheim who was stabbed to death last night."

"Yeah?"

"She was a friend of mine. I would like to know what they've got."

"For Christ's sake, how many times do I have to tell you to keep out of stuff like that and let the city handle it."

"I know," said the private detective, "I know. But she was a good friend. We were supposed to have dinner together last night." He lit a Marlboro and lost the thread of what he was saying. "Uh, I was there when they found her. Do what you can, will you?"

21

"Okay. I have to be downtown later. There's a new Greek restaurant near you on Broadway. I know that it's open today. Meet me there at one o'clock. Lunch is on you. Merry Christmas."

"Sure," Hardy answered, "Merry Christmas."

His left leg was aching. He massaged it for a bit and then said, "Holmes, you want to go out?"

The poodle started dancing around in anticipation. Hardy went into the foyer. Holmes was there before him, tugging at his leash, which was hanging from the coat rack on the wall. Hardy took a jacket from one of the hooks and put it on. Then he attached the dog's leash and they went out.

The gray snow was on its way to becoming slush. Hardy cursed at the slippery and placed his crutches very carefully. He thought about going back to the apartment and staying in till spring. "Goddamn it, Holmes, stop pulling."

The animal looked up at him with a big dog smile and kept straining toward the park.

While Holmes romped through a patch of virgin snow, Hardy smoked a cigarette and tried not to think of Kate.

He thought of her. He whistled the dog to him, and they went back to the building. They went to the main entrance to pick up the mail he had forgotten to collect the day before, and to complain about the snow not being shoveled away. "And tell them to put down a lot of salt. It gets slick as hell out there."

"I'll tell them, Mr. Hardy," said Pete, the doorman.

"Thanks," he answered, thinking about all the Christmas envelopes he had given out.

In the apartment Hardy brewed coffee and fortified it with brandy. The short outing had tired him more than he thought it would. He sipped his coffee and closed his eyes. The sound of shovels scraping concrete woke him. Twelve thirty. He finished off the cold coffee.

Outside men were shoveling away. "Don't forget the salt," he said to them and started the same trip he had made the night before, toward Broadway.

The trip was uneventful but tiring. Friday was already seated when Hardy got to the restaurant. The black cop eyed the crutches. "What happened to you? And why didn't you tell me about it, I could have come to your place."

Hardy dropped into the chair next to him. "I wanted to impress you with my bravery."

"I'm impressed. What happened?"

"After that little go-to on Fire Island, the leg kept tricking out, so my doctor decided I should have it operated on, and I did." The waiter was at their table. "Do you have beet salad? I'll have beet salad. Do you have egg and lemon soup?"

The waiter looked at him in surprise. "I'll see. Anything else?"

"Yes," said Hardy, "moussaka, and then I'll have some baklava and Greek coffee."

Friday shook his head. "If that's lunch, what do you have for dinner? Never mind, I don't want to know. I'll have the beet salad and the broiled brains . . . with pilaf and American coffee."

The waiter nodded and went.

Hardy had to do without his egg and lemon soup, but the rest of the meal was fine. The two men ate in silence. They both lit cigarettes to go with their coffee. Hardy sighed and nodded his approval of the meal. "What did you find out?"

"Not much," said Friday. "Too soon for the coro-

23

ner's report, and they haven't had a chance to talk to everyone yet. All I have is that she was stabbed to death. The names and address of the two guys she worked for. The names of the people who lived in the building. The owner and his wife, first floor, were out visiting. The guy next to the victim had a girlfriend in his apartment, and his mind was only on one thing. Nobody's talked to the two guys who live on the top floor yet. I typed it all up, here. When I get more, I'll let you know. Come on, I'll drive you home."

When he got home, Hardy pinned the piece of paper Friday had given him to the cork wall next to his desk and flicked on the TV. Christmas stuff. He turned the set off.

He had a headache. He took two aspirin and a tranquilizer and sat in the barber chair and slept. When he awoke, his leg ached.

Almost five o'clock. He took meat out for Holmes' dinner and wondered what he would have. A can of corned beef hash seemed the simplest solution. He took two more aspirin and emptied the hash into a frying pan. Second thoughts made him throw it all away, and he opened a can of tuna fish instead. He ate the fish out of the can with the help of several slices of white bread. His stomach protested, but he paid no attention to it. When he was through, he fixed himself a scotch and water and turned on the TV again. More Christmas. Off.

His eyes wandered over the titles on the shelves of his bookcase. *Thirty Years of Treason*. He never had finished that. *Around the World in Eighty Days*. Just the thing. He took it down and sat on the chaise. When he found himself reading the same paragraph over and over, he put the book down in disgust.

The evening passed and so did the night and so did

the next day. When a week had gone by, Hardy was thinking more about his knee than what had happened to Kate. At least he was trying to. The newspaper stories of her murder had evolved into stories of her rape and murder. But when newer and more interesting things happened in the world, the newspapers paid less attention to Kate, and Hardy wanted to do the same. The envelope Friday had sent lay unopened on his desk.

He read and he ate and he watched TV.

Soon the bandages were off, and he was bending his knee. He was making progress. But the police weren't. They still didn't know who had killed Kate.

Each day he took hot baths and bent the knee a little more.

Years before, when he had discovered that he made out better when he was thin than when he was fat, he had the room next to his bedroom made into a gym. It came in handy now. After his bath he went into the gym and worked out, concentrating on his left leg.

January became February, and Hardy put away his crutches and started using a cane. The police still hadn't come up with Kate's killer.

Hardy walked aimlessly about the apartment. He still thought about her. He felt he should do something, but he really didn't want to. He didn't want to get involved in murder. That was the police's job . . . why the hell weren't they doing it?

In one corner of his office there was a lectern which held a large dictionary. He found himself in front of the always open book and started leafing through it. He stopped to examine the word *chalybeate* when the phone rang.

"Hello."

"Is this 'Trouble Limited'?"

25

"Yes. Partrick Hardy speaking."

"Mr. Hardy, my name is Gold. Ernest Gold. I'm a furrier, and somebody is stealing furs out of my showroom, one or two a week. It's driving me crazy. I don't know how they're doing it. The security people in my building can't figure it out either. Maybe you could come take a look?"

"Sorry, Mr. Gold, I'm involved in a case that's taking all my time right now."

"Oh."

"Sorry. Goodbye."

Why did he do that? He hadn't worked since before the operation. He thought about looking Mr. Gold up in the telephone book and calling him back and taking the job. He wandered out of his office and about the living room as he considered the whys and why nots of calling Gold back.

The biggest why not was inescapable. He couldn't do anyting until he found who had murdered Kate Arnheim.

Chapter Four

The next morning after a workout and a shower, Hardy sat in the kitchen eating granola and sausages and eggs and preparing himself to open the envelope Friday had sent.

He moved to the living room and a wing chair with his second cup of coffee and the envelope. *TV Guide* was on the table next to the chair. Hardy put his cup down next to it and considered checking out the morning's movies.

"Shit," he said, and opened the envelope.

There was no salutation. It simply began:

"Somewhere between six and nine p.m. on December 24th, Kate Arnheim received multiple stab wounds. She died after 10:05 (you talked to her on the phone) and before 10:47 (when you and the patrolmen found her) due to loss of blood and shock as a result of those stab wounds. Traces of semen lead us to believe that the victim engaged in intercourse prior to the assault. It might have been with her killer. If it was the killer, he has type B blood (we got that from the semen), but that's not too much help since by a freak coincidence you and all the men living in the building have type B blood. So on that bit of circumstantial evidence we can't eliminate any one of you. Other things do, though.

"Henry Pritchett (the owner of the building) and his wife, Roberta, (they live on the first floor) were at a party in the Bronx. Plenty of witnesses.

"The deceased's next door neighbor, David Bishop, was shacked up in his apartment from five o'clock on. He and his girlfriend, Denise Shaw, say they think they heard something around eight o'clock. She says she's not sure. He says they heard something, but in New York who notices those things, and besides, he was busy.

"The two guys on the third floor, Ronald Fried and Ted McLean, alibi each other. Fried had called in sick at work and McLean had Christmas Eve day off. They said McLean was looking after Fried and keeping him company during the time that concerns us. They say they didn't hear anything. (The cop who talked to them told me they're both fags and were probably busy keeping each other company the same way David Bishop and his girlfriend kept each other company.)

"Your story checks out. (Yes, we checked you.)

"The Pritchetts own an antique shop on Amsterdam Avenue called 'Odds and Ends.'

"David Bishop is a press agent with an office on Eighth Avenue. His girlfriend is an actress, lives in the Village.

"Ronald Fried is a bookkeeper for a plumbing supply house downtown.

"Ted McLean is an assistant manager in a supermarket on the East Side.

28

"The deceased worked for two writers, Gary Thorpe and Ralph Price. Neither of them has type B blood, but we don't know that it was her killer who made it with her. They wrote that movie *Tony and Cleo, 1999*. Their office is on Fifty-eighth Street.

"There is one man we can't account for. The guy who was taking care of her. Thorpe and Price didn't pay her that much, and the clothes in her closet didn't come from Klein's bargain basement. The man who kept her is not fact, just theory.

"Kate Arnheim's mother, Madeline Bower (remarried, first husband dead), lives with her husband Carl just the other side of the river in Fort Lee, New Jersey.

"There was a holder for a letter opener and scissors on the desk in the living room. The scissors were still there, the letter opener was not. We figure the letter opener was the weapon that made all those stab wounds. We couldn't find it.

"With all that blood we figured the killer would have gotten some of it on him and left traces. Not a thing. No fingerprints. No footprints. There were some particles of dried blood on the bathroom floor (her type), but we couldn't find a thing in the tub or sink.

"That's it. Except for the junkie or weirdo or burglar who could have wandered in, killed her and left.

"Now that I've been dumb enough to send this to you, do us both a favor and tear it up and forget about it."

There was no signature. Hardy smiled an agreement of the common sense of Friday's closing remark and pinned the two typewritten sheets of paper to the cork wall.

He yawned and thought about how nice it would

be to take a nap. It was a good idea, but not the one he needed. Instead, he went to the bathroom and washed his face with cold water. Holmes frisked about in readiness as Hardy got dressed, then he barked his annoyance when he saw he wasn't going along.

Outside, Hardy took a deep breath of the cold, dry air and started walking uptown. He had no particular plan, but he thought that meandering around the neighborhood where Kate had lived might lead to something. It wasn't much, but it was all he had. Besides, walking was good for his leg.

It was empty on the Drive. He looked around to make sure that no one was watching and tried to twirl his cane. He dropped it. Looking around again, he picked up the cane and continued on his way.

He wandered around the Eighties between Riverside Drive and Broadway for almost an hour until his leg began to ache. On Broadway he stopped for a slice of pizza and a paper and then walked past Kate's building on his way to the bus. His only thought about the tough-looking dude with three rings on one hand and four on the other was that he was strange.

He saw him again the second day of his walking tour. What bothered Hardy was that the strange fellow with the rings was watching him.

He spent most of the third day watching television and preparing a lime meringue pie and filets of flounder in shrimp sauce. By the time the pie was chilling in the refrigerator and all the ingredients for the seafood dinner were ready for cooking, it was after five. Regretfully, Hardy left all this for another trip around the Eighties. He had waited until evening, or so he told himself, because he thought he might see something at night that wouldn't be evident during the daytime.

Actually, his friend with the rings was making Hardy nervous, and he hoped by going later he could avoid him.

No such luck. There was an alley just before Kate's building. As he went by an arm reached out and circled his neck. It was dark, but he could see the rings glittering in the light of the street lamp as the hand went under his jaw.

Hardy's reflexes went into action. The trouble was his body wasn't up to his reflexes. As soon as the arm encircled his neck, Hardy tucked his chin into his chest and started bending his knees in order to throw his attacker. But that damned left knee wouldn't bend enough . . . and it wouldn't hold his weight. As the pain from his uncooperating leg and his anguished throat vied for his attention, Hardy's reflexes switched signals. He put all his weight on his good leg and slashed back with his cane.

The blow was enough to make the man release his hold on Hardy, but that was all it did. Hardy turned to face a fist full of rings. He bobbed his head and hopped to his right. As he moved, he shoved the cane between his assailant's legs. The man was down, surprised, but not hurt . . . and the cane had snapped, leaving Hardy with only a splintered handle. Hardy's back found a brick wall while his hand reached for a garbage-pail cover.

"Police. Police. Police," shouted a strange but welcome voice.

Ringed fingers faked a move at Hardy and then darted down the alley and over a wooden fence.

While Hardy was catching his breath and fighting back the nausea, a worried face peeked into the alley. The blond young man asked, "Are you all right?"

"Yeah, I'm fine. Were you the one who yelled?"

The young man nodded.

"Thanks," said Hardy, "I needed that."

The young man walked closer. "Are you sure you're all right?"

"I think I'd better sit down," said Hardy. "My cane's broken." And he threw the handle away. "Give me a hand to the stoop, will you?"

When he was seated on the steps of the brownstone and smoking a cigarette, Hardy said, "I owe you a lot, thank you."

"That's all right. I live upstairs. It's a bit of a climb, but if you want to call the police or lie down . . ."

"No," said Hardy, "I'll be all right. Thanks again . . . uh . . ."

"Ronald. Ronald Fried."

For a brief second Hardy contemplated not using his own name, but the confusion of aliases had fouled him up before. "Patrick Hardy." They shook hands.

"Oh," said Ronald Fried, "you were Kate's friend."

"Yes," Hardy answered.

"I was, too. It's this terrible city. Look what almost happened to you just now. Well . . . if you're all right, I'll be getting upstairs."

"I hate to bother you," said Hardy, "but could you help me to the corner so I can get a cab."

"Well . . . sure."

All the way to the corner Hardy was a little sorry he'd asked. It seemed to him that Fried was holding him a little closer than was necessary. He suffered in silence. When they got to the corner, "I'll be fine now," he said. "Thank you. I really appreciate it."

"That's all right, I . . ."

"Hello, Ronny." The greeting came from another young blond man who had just crossed the street.

"Oh hi, Ted. Uh. Patrick Hardy, Ted McLean. Mr. Hardy was a friend of Kate Arnheim's. I was just going upstairs when I saw some maniac trying to mug him in the alley."

"Sounds exciting," said Ted McLean.

"Ted is my next door neighbor," said Ronald Fried.

"Nice to have met you, there's a cab. Thanks again," Hardy paused and then purposely added, "Ronny."

He could feel McLean's angry eyes on him as he crawled into the cab. He didn't know why he had baited the two homosexuals and filed it away for something to discuss with his analyst if he ever went to one.

At home he fed Holmes and set the flounder to cooking. As the filets simmered, he took long drinks of a large scotch. He had another drink while he beat the egg yolks.

Holmes sat under the table while his master ate, hoping to get a bonus. Hardy washed down the flounder and the shrimp with white wine and started coffee perking to go with the pie.

While he gorged on the pie and drank the coffee, he deliberated about reporting the mugging attempt and decided it wasn't worth the hassle. He poured himself another cup of coffee. He hadn't the vaguest idea of what to do next.

Chapter Five

The next day was Thursday, the day Laura came to clean. Hardy was leaving as she came in.

"Good morning, Laura. If the phone rings, let the service pick up. I don't know what time I'll be back." He wanted to leave before she could ask him why he was using an umbrella as a cane.

"Mr. Hardy, that's your umbrella . . ."

"I know, Laura. Thank you. Have a nice day."

"He's leaving you, Holmes."

This started the dog barking, which was what Laura had in mind.

Hardy made a face at her. "Very funny. Holmes, shut up. Goodbye, Laura."

"Goodbye." And she laughed as Holmes kept barking.

Fifteen minutes went by without a bus, then three of them showed up in a row. Hardy let the first two pass in order to get a seat on the third one.

The bus dropped him on Fifty-seventh Street, across the street from the cane shop.

The sword cane the old man showed him was tempting and appealed to Hardy's secret fantasies of himself as Errol Flynn. He settled for a strong walking stick made of oak. The sun was shining and it was a nice day. Also, he was within walking distance of Kate's former bosses and her next-door neighbor. The writers were the closest on West Fifty-eighth Street.

The lobby directory told him that they were on the ninth floor.

On nine, past the two-door offices of a lawyer, and a theatrical agent, and an importer, was a little alcove with a single door which had the number of the office and the two names: Gary Thorpe and Ralph Price. He opened the door and looked in.

There was no one at the desk. There were two doors behind it. He went to the one on the right and opened it and said, "Hello." There was no one inside to answer him. He attempted the same routine with the door on the left. He had the door open and his mouth was forming the word *hello* when he realized the two people on the couch were not interested in his greeting. The man looked up from the writhing, nude female body beneath him and stared at Hardy. Hardy didn't know whether the look on the man's face denoted surprise or anger or sexual climax. The private detective would have liked to watch the girl a while but decided against it and closed the door. He walked to the outside door to leave, but had second notions and sat down to wait.

Several old copies of *Time* and *Newsweek* later, the door on the left opened and the girl came out. Much to his disappointment, she was fully dressed. He had noticed the large breasts before, the rest of her was pretty nice, too. She couldn't have been more than eighteen.

36

His presence surprised her. She ran her fingers through her short black hair and said, "Oh, you startled me. I didn't hear you come in."

Hardy stifled several wise remarks and said, "Could I see Gary Thorpe or Ralph Price please."

"Do you have an appointment?"

"No, my name is Patrick Hardy, and I was wondering . . ."

The door on the left opened again. "I'm Gary Thorpe. Come on in, Mr. Hardy. Type those letters up right away, Frances."

"Yes, Gary."

Hardy closed the door. Gary Thorpe looked at him in an exaggerated manner and said, "The last time I ever saw a man with a walking stick and an umbrella . . . on a sunny day, was in an old and bad English movie."

Hardy sat opposite Thorpe's desk and hooked the umbrella over the arm of the chair. "I saw the movie. Wasn't that bad."

Thorpe grinned. "Despite the circumstances of our meeting, I might like you. We'll have to see what happens. What can I do for you?"

"Kate Arnheim."

"That's why your name connected. You're the guy who found Kate."

Hardy nodded.

The writer was about to say something else when his door opened. The balding black man standing in the doorway said, "Just wanted to let you know I was back." He started to close the door.

"Wait a minute, Ralph," said Thorpe. "This is Pat Hardy. Pat, this is my partner, Ralph Price."

Hellos were exchanged and Thorpe said, "Pat was the one who found Kate Arnheim that night."

"Oh," said Ralph Price, and he pulled out a pipe and a tobacco pouch. "What can we do for you?"

"I'm a private detective and since I'm personally involved and the police don't seem to be getting anywhere, I thought I'd dig around and see what I could come up with."

After carefully tamping the tobacco, Price lit his pipe. He drew in some smoke and let it out and shook his head and laughed. "Excuse my reaction, but Gary and I once wrote that speech for a detective in one of our movies. We had to throw it out because it didn't work. And here you are saying it to me and it works fine."

"Very interesting," said the private detective, "could you tell me anything . . ."

"Look, Mr. Hardy, Gary and I are involved in a new project, and I'm afraid we don't have much time. Kate worked for us. We both dated her, and we both slept with her."

It seemed to Hardy that the black man was waiting for some sort of reaction from him. He didn't give him any. Price continued, "More than that we can't tell you. Gary, I'll be in my office." And he left.

Hardy put his new walking stick to the floor and rose from the chair.

"Wait a minute, Pat," said Thorpe. "You haven't got it quite straight. Kate wasn't like Fran out there. There were no quick bounces on the boss's couch for her. Sure, I dated her. Sure, Ralph dated her. But when he did, he told me he was stuck on her and that she liked him, too. So I stayed out of their way. They had a good thing going, too, until about two months before she died. Ralph only acted that way because your showing up reminded him of what happened and kind of hit him where he lives."

Hardy retrieved his umbrella. "Thanks for your time, Mr. Thorpe."

"Gary, please."

"Gary. Sorry to bother you."

In the outer office Hardy gave a quick longing glance at Frances and left.

It was almost one o'clock.

He had intended to visit David Bishop, whose office was only several blocks away on Eighth Avenue, but toting around both the walking stick and the umbrella was annoying, and he simply couldn't see throwing the umbrella away.

The cabdriver who took him home said, "Thank you," and "Have a nice day." Hardy took the man at his word and got lost in the problems of Marlene Dietrich in *Dishonored*. When Marlene's problems were disposed of, he started to make dinner and was prepared to bury himself in his food and whatever television had to offer.

His intentions were clear. He was going to have a good day. But Ralph Price wouldn't let him. The man's attitude had rubbed him the wrong way. Hardy had tried to suppress his feelings, but they wouldn't suppress. He picked up the kitchen phone and dialed Manhattan North.

"Friday speaking."

"Hello, it's Pat. I . . ."

"How the hell did you know?"

"Know what?"

"If this is a coincidence, it sure is strange. David Bishop's body was discovered on the floor of his office. Somebody shot him through the head."

"I'll be damned."

"That would be nice."

"What time did it happen?" Hardy asked.

39

"He was alive and well about twelve o'clock, his body was discovered at a little after two, you figure it out."

"That's interesting. Ralph Price was out of his office till just before one o'clock. I wonder where he was?"

"I suppose you think he killed the girl, too."

"Maybe. How was his alibi for Christmas Eve?"

"Not the best. He says he spent it alone in his apartment. No one saw him. But Gary Thorpe's alibi isn't much better. He says he was supposed to go to a party, but fell asleep on the couch in his office. When he woke up it was Christmas Day. Nobody saw him leave the building. But neither one of them has the right blood type. You know that."

"Balls," Hardy answered. "You said yourself it didn't have to be her killer who made it with her. How do you know everybody's blood type anyway? You didn't take samples."

"It's the modern age," said Friday. "We have a computer that's in touch with other computers, like the Army's, for instance. Let's just say the information is available. Big Brother is watching you."

"Well, Big Brother could be wrong. It happened to me, remember. Some clown in the Army had me classified as type O when all the time I was type B."

"We double-check," said Friday. "The Red Cross keeps records, too. Is there anything else?"

"Yeah. Find out where Price was today."

"You are really hot to nail him, aren't you? There are two completely different m.o.'s involved. It could be that Bishop's death isn't even connected with the girl's."

"It could be, but I doubt it, and so do you. At least

40

until it's checked out. Why are you so adamant that Price didn't do it?"

"Maybe for the same reason you're so sure he did. We both have our prejudices, only I know about mine."

"Wait a minute," Hardy protested.

"You wait a minute. And think about it. Maybe the fact that a black man made it with a girl you were screwing galls you more than you would like to say, even to yourself."

"Come on, Friday. I knew Kate went with a lot of guys, all shapes and colors."

"Sure," said the policeman. "Sure, you accepted it as a generality, but as a specific, it bugs hell out of you. Admit it, you wouldn't be so set on him if he were white. Now if you don't mind, I've got work to do. Goodbye, Private Detective."

Hardy started to answer, but there was no one on the line. He hung up the phone and leaned against the table and thought about what Friday had said.

"No," he said with certainty, after a few minutes. "He's full of it." And he cut an avocado open and put bacon on to fry. Tonight's first course was guacamole.

The next day's newspaper didn't tell him much more than he knew. But David Bishop was the police's problem. Even if his killing did figure in Kate's death, the professionals were better equipped to check it out than Hardy was. Or Kate's death, too, for that matter. With the acceptance of that fact, he pondered what to do next. The papers from the cork wall gave him three choices: Henry and Roberta Pritchett, Carl and Madeline Bower, and Denise Shaw. Since the police would probably be talking to the press agent's girlfriend about his death, Hardy relegated Denise Shaw to another time.

41

He realized that what he wanted was confirmation of his suspicions about Ralph Price. Friday's remarks replayed themselves and nagged at him. He pushed them out of his mind and decided that Kate's mother and stepfather would be his best bet.

He knew he could never bend his knee enough to be comfortable in his VW. It would have to be by bus. He got up from his desk to get a drink of water. Holmes was sleeping on the chaise. Hardy looked at the dog with envy and went back to his desk to dial the phone.

"Directory Assistance."

"Ma'am, a listing for Port Authority information."

"Certainly, at the George Washington Bridge or One hundred and . . ."

"I'm sorry, the bus terminal."

"Forty-first? Information?"

"Yes."

She gave him the number, which he dialed. When the new voice came on the line, he told it where he wanted to go.

"Are you leaving from Midtown Terminal?"

"Yes."

"The Black and Green line has a bus that leaves at eleven ten."

"He looked at his watch, "And after that?"

"At eleven forty and at twelve ten."

Hardy thanked her and hung up the phone. Then he stuck his tongue out. He really didn't want to go.

The Port Authority Bus Terminal in midtown Manhattan was in its normal organized chaotic state: the cabs stopped only long enough to load and unload, and the kids hustled bags. Hardy entered from the Eighth Avenue side. He bought a *Playboy* at the newsstand and looked at the different disciples lined

42

against the wall. Birchers and Communists and Zionists and Arabs and Republicans and Democrats and Children for Jesus and People for Legal Marijuana, all coexisted in semi-civility while teams of blacks, aloof from the wall-sitters, flanked the steep escalators and sold their newspapers . . . and the Hari Krishna people wandered about smiling.

Blacks and whites and other shades in between went along their various ways. Hardy bought a round-trip ticket and went to the platform to wait for his bus. He knew it was silly not to call the Bowers beforehand, but he was doing it anyway.

He sat in the rear seat so he would have room for his legs. He was there before he knew it. When the bus stopped, he asked the driver if he knew where 251 Elm Avenue was.

"Sorry, pal, all I know about this town is this spot right here. I'm from Brooklyn myself."

Hardy walked to the corner and saw that he was on Elm Avenue. It was another half mile before he was at 251. He started up the driveway and a voice said, "They ain't there."

Hardy looked and saw that the voice came from the garage of the next house. He walked toward it.

"You looking for the Bowers?" said the man.

"Yes," said Hardy, "do you know when they'll be back."

"Ain't coming back. They moved to California. Two weeks ago."

Chapter Six

When he got home more than two hours later, he hadn't had any lunch and was feeling annoyed and very sorry for himself. "Come on, Holmes, get up. You're sleeping your life away."

The poodle kept its place on the chaise and snuggled in to go back to sleep. Until he heard the refrigerator open.

"I knew that would get you up," said Hardy as he put a bowl of cold noodles almandine on the electric warmer. "What do you want?"

Holmes stared with soulful eyes. Hardy laughed and opened the refrigerator again and took out Holmes's vitamins. "Sit. That's it." The tablet was gone in a gulp. "No more," said Hardy and he went to the phone. When he got Friday on the line, "Did you know that Kate's parents moved to California two weeks ago?"

"Yes."

"Why the hell didn't you tell me?"

"You didn't ask me. Goodbye."

Hardy slammed the phone down. He ate the noodles cold and poured himself some scotch. While he drank, it occurred to him that he was horny. He hadn't made it with anyone since Kate. It hadn't bothered him until now, but now it was bothering him a lot.

He made several phone calls. Zero.

He looked up Denise Shaw's phone number. True, she was probably being bombarded by the police about Dave Bishop, but if he could kill two birds with one stone . . . ?

He dialed.

"Hello."

"Denise Shaw?"

"That's me."

"My name is Patrick Hardy. I was a friend of Dave Bishop and . . ."

"I was, too. Isn't it terrible what happened to poor David?"

"Yes, it is."

"Okay."

"Okay, what?" said Hardy.

"Well, I don't want to dwell too long on David's death. Things like that are so depressing. I don't want you to think I'm an insensitive person, it's just that if you can't change things by words, why bother with the words . . . so I don't want to talk about David any more . . . okay? What else do you want to talk about?"

Hardy wasn't too sure if he understood all of that. At a loss to say anything else he said, "I was wondering if you would like to have dinner with me."

"Okay."

"Okay," Hardy parroted.

"I'll be ready at seven." She gave him her address and hung up.

He chewed on his lip as he tried to figure out what had just happened. Nothing figured. He decided to wait and see and ran himself a tub.

The bath made him very sleepy, and he wished he could merely call the girl up and tell her to join him in bed, but since that wasn't the way of it, he got dressed. It was too early so he attempted to make some sense of the "investigation" so far. All he had when he was through was his original list of people with David Bishop and the Bowers crossed out. This new list went up on the cork wall.

It was still early. Hardy prepared Holmes's dinner. Then he turned on the television and turned it off. He looked through his own TV scanner that covered the street entrance. Nothing interesting. He swiveled around in his chair and looked up at the shelves of books. He got up to take a closer look. Muhammad Ali's face stared at him from the paperback cover of *Sting Like a Bee*. Hardy took the book to the chaise and read till it was time to go.

On the subway downtown he thought about the book and realized that he didn't understand violent people. Every time he faced violence it scared him and sickened him. The Army had taught Patrick Hardy how to deal with violence physically, but they hadn't been able to do anything about the fear that clutched at his gut when he was forced to face it.

Boxers had it. Most athletes had it. His friend Steve Macker had it. That ability to come eyeball to eyeball with violence and not be afraid. Not Patrick Hardy. Even now he was a little nervous simply thinking about it.

When the train stopped at West Fourth Street, he

47

had replaced those thoughts with images of what Denise Shaw was going to be like.

Over to Sullivan Street and up three flights, and he would know.

Climbing stairs was still no fun. He waited a minute until his breath came back to him, and he knocked at the door.

"Hi, come on in . . . you look pretty good for a phone pick-up."

"You're not bad yourself," he answered, enjoying her frankness. She didn't have the large chest he usually favored, but she had enough. She was a small pixie-like girl with short red hair and green eyes and sparkling teeth.

Denise Shaw was checking him out, too, and she had noticed the walking stick and his limp. "I'm ready to go, unless you want to have a drink here. All I have is red wine, but if you want to rest for a while, I mean because of your leg . . . I've never gone out with a cripple before. I'm sorry. That's the wrong word to use, isn't it? Doesn't turn me off on you though. Might even be a turn-on. Is that kinky?"

"Might be," he laughed. "But stop worrying about it. I had an operation on my knee in December. In another month I won't even need this stick."

"Oh, that's good."

"Get your coat."

"Okay."

In the cab uptown she questioned him nonstop. "How tall are you?"

"Six feet."

"How much do you weigh?"

"One hundred and eighty pounds." He lied by five pounds.

"What's your sign?"

"Capricorn . . . what is this with these questions?"

She leaned closer, her hand on his arm. "You have brown eyes." Her hand squeezed his arm. "And you have muscles. I am five foot two, eyes of green. I weigh one hundred pounds, and I'm an Aquarius . . . and I don't have muscles . . . well I do have muscles, but I'm soft. There . . . I like to get all the small talk out of the way quickly so we can talk about real things. Think about it and you'll see that I'm right."

"I don't have to think about it. You are right."

"Okay," and keeping a firm grasp on his arm, she leaned back to enjoy the rest of the ride.

Nero's Steakhouse was in the West Forties. When the cab pulled up, Denise squeezed his arm tighter. "Nobody ever took me here before, oh boy, Pat me boy, you sure know how to treat a lady."

He laughed and paid off the cabdriver. The restaurant was located on the second floor, atop a flight of stairs, no elevator. Hardy had forgotten that. There was a wait for a table so they went to the bar for a drink. Hardy leaned against a stool, grateful for the chance to rest his knee. "Cutty Sark, please. Straight up. Water on the side."

"Same thing," Denise said to the bartender, "but mix mine."

Hardy drank the shot of scotch in one gulp and motioned to the bartender for another. He drank part of the second shot and sipped his water. "What are some of the real things you want to talk about?"

"Now don't be mean," said Denise, and she took the swizzle stick out of the glass and tasted her drink. "That's the kind of question I don't like."

49

"Sorry," said Hardy. "You want real and you want honest."

"Right."

"All right," he said, "honest it is. No small talk."

Her eyes twinkled at him over her glass.

"The most honest thing I can think of," he said, "is that after dinner I would like to take you straight home and straight to bed."

"That's nice. Are you sure you can wait until after dinner?"

"Let's go now, if you want."

"No," she said. "Sometimes it's more fun if you wait."

He was saved from having to come up with the right response by the maitre d' telling them their table was ready.

He enjoyed the lobster, but as they ate and sucked the meat out of the shell, Hardy visualized them in the eating scene from *Tom Jones*.

He drained his coffee. "Ready to go?"

Her mouth formed a pout, then a smile. "I'd like a brandy."

They sipped their Grand Marnier and he looked at her while she looked around.

"Oh," she said as the star of a Broadway show walked in, "there's Jack . . ."

But Hardy wasn't listening. Seated midway between them and the entering star were Gary Thorpe and Ralph Price. Price was having an animated discussion with a third man who was standing over them.

"Tell me, Miss Rubberneck, do you know them?"

"The good-looking one with the three-hundred-dollar suit is James Victor Norse. The other two are somebodies, but I don't know who."

"They wrote *Tony and Cleo, 1999*," said Hardy. "Who the hell is James Victor Norse, and how do you know his suit cost three hundred dollars?"

"I saw that movie. I liked it. There was one scene . . ."

"Denise . . . James Victor Norse. Who is he?"

"You're putting me on. He's everything. Money. All crooked. He has an office on Park Avenue. Very legitimate, investment counselor or something like that, but he's supposed to have his finger in every racket there is. Nobody's ever proved it, and he's never even been arrested. Very well connected with the Organization. Everybody knows that."

"I didn't."

"Could I have another brandy? Of course his suit cost three hundred dollars. If you had his money, wouldn't your suits cost three hundred dollars? Only logical."

Norse by this time had pulled up a chair at the writers' table and was continuing his conversation with Ralph Price. Gary Thorpe was paying attention to his dinner.

When Hardy and Denise finished their second brandy and he had paid the check, he debated passing close to Price's and Thorpe's table. Gary Thorpe solved his problem.

"Pat. Over here. You know Ralph, and this is James Norse. Patrick Hardy."

Price and Norse glared at Thorpe and then nodded a curt hello to Pat and Denise and took their conversation to a whisper. Thorpe, oblivious to their displeasure, was busy ogling Denise.

"Denise Shaw . . . Gary Thorpe . . ." Hardy was stopped from going on by the sound of Norse's chair scraping as he stood up. A cursory nod at everybody and he was gone.

Hardy picked up his sentence, ". . . and Ralph Price."

They both said hello, but Thorpe pursued it. "You're a very pretty girl, Denise. Are you an actress?"

"As a matter of fact, I am."

"Very interesting. You might be right for a picture we're doing. What do you think, Ralph?"

Price nodded, helping Thorpe make his pitch. "Could be."

"Why don't you call me," said Thorpe. "I'll give you my number."

"I've got your number, Gary," said Hardy, and he started maneuvering Denise toward the exit. "I'll give it to her."

As they went down the stairs to the street, Denise demanded, "Why the hell did you rush me out of there like that? You're very possessive."

"I hope you weren't falling for that line of bull. All he wants to do is get laid."

"Well, that's all you want, too, but at least with him I might get a chance at a part in a movie."

They stood outside not speaking as the doorman went for a cab. Hardy noticed Norse getting into a limousine. There was something familiar about the chauffeur, Hardy thought, but he was more concerned about dealing with Denise.

They got into the taxi. The ride downtown was frosty, tense and silent. When they arrived, Hardy started to say something. Denise cut him off. "Don't be a jerk. I blow up fast and I forget fast. Come on up."

In the apartment she took his walking stick and

coat and put them in a closet. "We both know you're going to stay a while, so why be coy." The last she punctuated with a soft warm kiss. "Don't go away, I'll get the wine."

Her hair smelled good as she snuggled close to him on the couch. "Do me a favor," she said. "Slow. No rush job, please. I can't stand slam, bam, thank you ma'am. Take it easy."

He kissed her slowly and gently and though his groin ached, he managed to confine himself to prolonged and innocent necking until . . . "When I said slow, I didn't mean forever, but you're sweet and I love you for it. Help me out of this thing, will you. You have such soft gentle hands. Not many men are as considerate as you are."

The sight of her small breasts was not a disappointment. In fact, their dainty perfection aroused him even more. As he bent his head to kiss them, a vague thought of puppies with pink noses ran through his head.

They were taking off the rest of their clothes when a frantic limb knocked over a wine glass.

"Forget it," she gasped, "you've been gentle long enough. Please. Now. Please."

They were quite good together, and the last thing he remembered before they both dozed was her tongue in his ear and a faint "thank you."

Hardy delayed his ego-tripping sleep long enough to answer, "Thank you." And in that mini-second before he slept, it dawned on him that James Victor Norse's chauffeur was also his many-ringed friend from the alley.

Chapter Seven

When he awoke Denise was standing across the room looking in a mirror. With the exception of a pair of black boots, she was nude. She was touching her nipples with her fingers.

"Good morning," she said. "What do you think? Is this a turn-on?"

"Huh?"

"This pose. I was thinking of getting some nude shots taken. Does what I'm doing turn you on?"

"Come here and find out."

"Before breakfast?"

"Instead of."

This time he wasn't slow and gentle about it, but she didn't seem to mind.

Later she served him terrible black coffee and examined them both in the mirror. "That would make an interesting shot. Would you pose with me?"

"No thanks, Denny, I'm a very private person. Don't you have any milk?"

"I'm sorry. Never use it."

"How about something to eat," said Hardy, "I'm starving."

She shook her head and smiled and looked back at the mirror to see how she looked cupping her breasts with her hands. "That's cute."

"So are you. Get dressed and I'll buy you breakfast."

"Can't. I have a dance class and then a reading . . . are you going to give me Gary Thorpe's number?"

"Sure. Where are my pants?"

"I hung them up. I'll get them." She ran to the closet. When she came back, she had the pants draped in front of her. She checked this pose in the mirror, too. "No, that won't do it." Then abruptly, "Why did you call me?"

"To take you out . . . and hopefully what did happen."

"No, I mean besides that. What did David have to do with it?"

Hardy looked for a cigarette, found it, and lit it. "On Christmas Eve a friend of mine was stabbed to death . . ."

"Oh."

Hardy nodded. "You and Dave Bishop were next door that night. I thought the police would have come up with her killer by now . . . anyway, I was going to ask Dave Bishop about it, but I never got around to it."

"Do you think David's death had anything to do with your friend's?"

"Maybe yes, maybe no. It's hard to say."

She took a drag from his cigarette and put it back in his mouth. "That's what the police said. I couldn't tell them anything when they asked me about Christmas Eve. There was nothing serious between David and me, but you know me, when I get into it, I concentrate on what I'm doing, and that night we were really into it. I couldn't help them with David either. We hadn't seen each other in almost a month."

"You break up?"

"No. There was nothing to break up. He was busy with his thing, and I was into mine. You and your friend have something special going?"

"Sort of like you and Bishop, but Kate was a good friend, and since I am a private detective, it's only . . ."

"Are you really?"

"Yes," he said, cringing at her enthusiasm. "Don't make such a big deal out of it, it isn't. Actually, I'm not supposed to say detective—investigator."

"A private detective. What do you think? Does David's death have anything to do with Kate's?"

"Like I said, I don't know."

"Well, David was a friend of mine, and I'd like to help. . . . Oh, that's not true. It just sounds like it might be fun. Does that sound rotten?"

"No. Just honest. More than I could be. It's not as glamorous as you think. Most of the time you talk to people who don't know anything, and when you're through, you don't know anything."

"Then what happens?"

"You talk to someone else and repeat the process. If that sounds like fun to you . . ." He was about to invite her to tag along when a door in his brain opened and he re-remembered who Norse's chauffeur was.

"Go on."

"No, never mind. I'd better get some breakfast."

"Come on, Pat. You were about to tell me I could work on the case with you."

"It was a bad idea. Forget it."

"Please. Pretty please. If you say yes, I won't call Gary Thorpe."

He laughed and pulled her to his lap. "You can call him if you want, and yes, you can come along on some of my boring interviews."

"Oh, thank you." And she kissed him and squirmed around in his lap, which was a mistake. He never got any breakfast and she never got to her dance class.

A sidewalk hot dog vendor supplied their lunch. Afterward he dropped Denise off at her audition and decided to walk home along Madison Avenue.

His attention was caught by a window display of weighted belts used for exercising. The one for reducing the stomach wasn't too appealing, but he did like the idea of the two-pound weight that went around the ankle. It seemed like a good way to exercise without working at it. Something like that always interested Patrick Hardy.

He went in and bought the small black belt and wrapped it around the ankle of his bad leg. The velcro fastening made a snug and comfortable fit. After ten blocks of walking with it, he got tired so he flagged a cab to take him the rest of the way home. All in all, he was very pleased with himself.

Hardy had planned on visiting the Pritchetts, but since he was tired and today was Saturday anyway, he decided to let it go until Monday. Maybe he would call Denise, and they would go to the antique shop together.

In the apartment he listened to Holmes's barking argument and placated the dog with a quick tour through Riverside Park. Back inside, the two of them made for the chaise and fell asleep.

He awoke long enough to eat a bread and butter sandwich, turn up the heat, wash the lipstick stains out of his shirt with Woolite and take a bath. Then, wrapped in a towel, he went back to bed.

When he awoke this time, he turned on the TV and got dressed. Ty Power was trying to get the Suez Canal built while Hardy was trying to decide whether to settle for pea soup for dinner or to exert himself and prepare coquilles St. Jacques.

As he usually did when he saw an historical movie, Hardy went to the encyclopedia to check fact against fiction. Unfortunately, Ferdinand De Lesseps' real life wasn't as romantic as the one Power depicted in the movie. Disappointed, Hardy snapped the encyclopedia shut and watched the rest of the picture while he made both the soup and the coquilles.

He spent the rest of the weekend alone. Part of the time he reread Josephine Tey's *The Daughter of Time* and wished he could be like her hospitalized detective and solve all his problems from bed.

On Monday Denise called. "Do you want me to meet you someplace, or will you pick me up, or what?"

"Why don't you meet me here?" And he told her his address.

When he hung up, Hardy got undressed and into a pair of new pajamas and a robe. He had already had breakfast but he brewed a fresh pot of coffee in the electric percolator.

Coffee and cigarette in hand he sat in the barber chair and waited in anticipation.

Denise arrived all perky and cheerful and ready for her new adventure. She mentioned noticing Hardy's doormat that said Go Away and thought it was cute.

She remarked about all the locks on the door and what a great apartment it was.

She and Holmes got along fine.

When all that flurrying of coming in was done, she appraised Hardy in his pajamas and robe.

"I'll make you a bet you never wear pajamas." She didn't let him answer. "I'll make you another bet that you're horny."

He grinned like a little boy caught in the act.

"I'll think about it," she said and drank from his coffee cup. "That's good. Do you have any more?"

While he was pouring she said, "Where's the bedroom?"

He put down the pot and the cup. "You coming or do you want me to carry you?"

"Carry me. Just like in the movies."

His bad leg made it a bit difficult but he managed.

She was in a frolicking mood. When they were both naked and in bed, she hid under the covers. When he came after her, she tickled him and kept avoiding his grasp. They were rolling and giggling and . . . without a word they became very still. He put his hands to her waist and drew her to him, their bodies connecting at various important points.

Soon the sweet beginning changed into a frantic search for climax, and they moved and maneuvered for more complete contact. He was ready. But he could feel her desperation. They were slightly out of sync. She wasn't there yet. He waited. Waited. Waited. And her little grunts of despair stopped. He felt her throb and heard the low moan of joy that became a scream.

Sated, they didn't separate but slept as they were.

When he awoke she smiled at him. "I think my ribs are broken." And she kissed him.

They took a shower and had what was left of Saturday's pea soup for lunch while they watched *The Galloping Gourmet* showing how he prepared sponge finger biscuits with lemon-wine jelly and whipped cream.

They decided to walk uptown through the park. Holmes wanted to come along. Denise agreed with the poodle. Hardy vetoed the whole idea and they left. He glanced at the paper taped to the lamp post and started to cross the street, but Denise tugged his arm and made him read about someone offering a reward for his lost cat.

"Poor little thing," he said. "You're a detective, why don't you find it?"

"I'm working on another case."

"Cop-out," she said, and hugged herself closer to him as they walked.

The antique shop on Amsterdam Avenue was only a few blocks away from Kate's building. As they passed the building, Denise made a funny noise. Hardy looked at her questioningly. She shook her head and they kept walking.

His mind was everywhere. Back in bed with Denise. Back in bed with Kate. The fact of Kate's death. His suspicions about Ralph Price. What the Pritchetts were like. The man with rings on his fingers . . . Hardy made a bad mental joke . . . and bells on his toes. "Did you ever meet Ralph Price before Friday night?"

"Thorpe's partner? I didn't really meet him then. He hardly spoke two words to us."

"Well, did you ever hear Dave Bishop talk about him?"

"He might have, Pat, nothing that I remember. Why?"

61

"I don't know. There it is. 'Odds and Ends.' "

The shop lived up to its name. Ice cream chairs were stacked next to an imitation Chippendale piece, which was next to a Hitchcock potty chair. Various shelves and tables held pressed glass and Meissen ware and Coke trays and toy banks.

Hardy glanced through a pile of old sheet music. He had just come across a fairly good copy of "Ma" with Eddie Cantor's picture on the cover when Denise went into her act. She had lifted the cover on the potty chair and was exclaiming, "What a divine chair. Darling, we must have it."

Hardy cringed. He had assumed that Denise was a natural actress, and was in no way prepared for her being such an outrageous ham.

He nodded, hoping she would get the clue and shut up. She didn't. There were no other customers in the store. Hardy could see a man in the back writing in a ledger book. He assumed that was Mr. Pritchett. The slightly butch-looking plump blonde woman heading for Denise had to be Mrs. Pritchett.

Denise was going on. "Sweetheart, I just love this chair."

"They're very rare," the woman said in a deep voice. "Bette Davis collects them."

"Oh," said Denise, but before she could continue, Hardy broke in.

"How much is this sheet music?"

The woman turned to him. "Three dollars."

"I'll take it. Are you Mrs. Pritchett?"

"Yes, I am."

"My name is Patrick Hardy. My enthusiastic friend is Denise Shaw. I'm a private detective, and I'd like to ask you a few things about Kate Arnheim and David Bishop."

62

"Henry," she called to the man in the back, "could you come out for a moment?"

Henry and Roberta Pritchett were very nice and very patient and answered all of Hardy's questions. When they left the shop, he didn't know a bit more.

"Denny, what the hell was all that playacting about?"

"Sorry. I didn't know you would be so straightforward. I thought we were supposed to be customers and that they would be off their guard and tell us something that they wouldn't and . . ." Her voice trailed off into a wounded silence.

"That comes from seeing too many movies."

She didn't answer.

"Hey, I'm not mad. Forget it."

"Are you sure?"

"Positive."

"Prove it," she said.

"Okay. Come on back to my place."

"No, we can do that any time. Take me to the movies. That one across the street and buy me popcorn and soda and a candy bar."

"It's a deal."

They loaded up on supplies and since the movie house was almost empty, they had their choice of seats. They sat up front where they stuffed themselves and held hands and enjoyed the double feature.

Afterward they walked toward the Drive to take the bus downtown.

Hardy had assumed Denise was coming to his place. It surprised him when she told him she was going home.

"Okay," he said, playing it cool.

63

"If you must know, Gary Thorpe said he might call."

"Fine," he said.

"Okay," she answered.

"What are you so mad about? You said you were busy. All right, you're busy. You're a free human being. I've got no claim on you. I thought the new women hated possessive men."

"I am not one of the new women and I love possessive men."

They were passing Kate's building during this little tiff. Hardy was about to respond to Denise's last remark when he saw Ronald Fried coming down the stairs with a bag of garbage.

"Hi," he said to Hardy.

"Hello," Hardy answered. He planned to keep walking.

Denise tugged at his arm. "Who's that?" she whispered.

Fried was shoving his bag of garbage into a can.

"He lives in this building," said Hardy.

"He's a suspect, isn't he? Let's talk to him."

Hardy wanted to go, but by this time Fried had finished with his chore and had turned around. "How's your leg?"

"Coming along. Denise, this is Ronald Fried. Ron, Denise Shaw."

"Hi. Excuse me, I just got home from work, and I saw that I forgot to take the garbage out this morning. After all those stairs, I've got to go up and have a drink . . ."

Hardy couldn't categorize the look Fried was giving him, but he didn't like it. "Would you like to come up and join me?"

"Well . . ." said Hardy.

That's as far as he got. "We'd love to," said Denise, "unless the climb would be too much for your leg."

"No," said Hardy, "a drink sounds just fine."

"Oh good," said Fried, "I just love having company." He started up the stoop. As he turned, Hardy brandished his walking 'stick at Denise who made a face at him.

Despite her antics, he could tell that Denise was experiencing the same sort of feeling he was when they came to the second floor landing where Kate Arnheim and David Bishop had once lived.

"Not there, one more flight," Fried yelled from the next flight of stairs. He stopped and looked down at Hardy, "Oh, I'm sorry. I forgot for a moment."

"Yeah," Hardy answered. Denise took his hand and held it as they walked up the rest of the way.

Fried lived in the front apartment. Hardy was surprised to see that it was sedate and practical and not at all fruity.

Fried kept up a running conversation from the kitchen while he collected ice cubes and other paraphernalia.

Satisfied he wasn't coming back for a few seconds, Denise opened a closet and poked around. Hardy went to chase her away.

"Okay, you search, I'll go keep him busy," she said conspiratorially. "Wait a minute," she yelled to Fried, "I'll come in and help."

Her poking had knocked some things to the floor. Hardy picked them up and hung them back in the closet, straightening things out as best he could. As he pushed one final hanger back into place, he noticed the blue dress hidden under an overcoat in the corner. Someplace in his mind he smirked at fags and transvestites and closed the closet door.

They were coming back. He went to the window and lit a cigarette and looked out just in time to see the man with the rings going into the building directly across the street.

He drank his drink and the next one and nodded at the conversation that became progressively more faggy. Denise seemed to have a quality that made Fried relax. He seemed to like drinking and talking, and the more he drank, the more he talked. By the time they were ready to go, she and Ronny were close friends. Hardy was bored by it all, but it occurred to him that what Ronny really wanted was to be a close friend of his. But that wasn't his major concern. The man with the rings on his fingers was.

On the bus ride downtown Denise said something about it not really being important that she go home, and that she would love to come back with him, if the invitation was still open.

He knew he should say no. He had a lot of thinking to do. What was Rings doing across the street? Was James Norse involved? And did either one of them have anything to do with the death of Kate Arnheim or David Bishop. He should type that all up and pin it to his bulletin board. He should think about it and try to make it fall into place.

"Pat, your stop is next. What do I do?"

"What do you think?" he said as they rushed off the bus. "You come with me to the land of chicken breasts in cream sauce, old Humphrey Bogart movies, and not a wink of sleep all night long."

"Promises, that's all I get is promises," she said as they ran across the street.

Chapter Eight

In the morning she prattled away while they bathed and he worked out, and they breakfasted on pineapple juice and oatmeal and buckwheat cakes and bacon.

She called her service and found that she had a reading for a commercial that morning. Hardy had mixed emotions while she scurried around getting dressed and getting out. He enjoyed her company, but he enjoyed his own, too. Besides he had work to do.

When she was gone, he typed up the thoughts that had worried him the day before on the bus. Following that, he typed:

How to find out:

1. Visit the building across the street where Rings went in.

2. Visit James Victor Norse at his Park Avenue office.

3. Visit Gary Thorpe and Ralph Price and get

them to introduce me to James Victor Norse. (Price seems to be a friend of Norse's.)

Hardy pinned this new list to the cork wall and stared at it. Number one scared him to death. Number two was a possibility. Number three seemed like his best bet. Besides, it would give him another shot at Price. He stared at the wall.

Where was the dog?

"Holmes," he called out.

The dog didn't come. This wasn't normal. Hardy went into the bedroom. The poodle was sprawled in his own bed looking very much like a sad old man.

Hardy checked his nose. "You're fine. Come on. What's wrong with you?"

Then he remembered. It had happened before. There was nothing physically wrong with the animal. He had picked up Hardy's vibrations. Since Hardy was feeling nervous and out of sorts, Holmes automatically felt the same way. Hardy scratched his friend behind the ear, and assured him that everything was all right. Holmes looked at him doubtfully but enjoyed the scratching.

For the dog's sake as well as his own, Hardy set out cold cuts, cheeses, and rye bread and a bottle of wine and escaped away the day watching game shows and old movies.

On Wednesday after his workout, he decided to leave the two-pound weight strapped to his ankle. He hardly noticed it, and it was a painless way of strengthening the leg.

With that decision out of the way, he thought about his other problems. He pulled the receiver of the phone out of the ice bucket where he had stuffed it the night before and checked with his service. Denny had called. That was it.

He called her, but she wasn't home. He dialed the phone again and left word with her service.

His problems were still there to be dealt with. Absent-mindedly he thumbed through *TV Guide* then dramatically threw the magazine across the room. Holmes pounced on it and reduced it to a mass of shredded paper. Objects at rest were verboten, but anything thrown was fair game.

Hardy watched the animal at play, envying him. Then he worried that now he would have to buy a new *TV Guide* and that he would have to pick up the mess that was being made. His eyes shifted from Holmes to the cork wall.

"Crap," he said, and he left the apartment in order to visit the writers' office.

It seemed like a contradiction, but the combination of the leg weight and the walking stick worked out very well. Impatiently Hardy left the Riverside Drive bus stop and went over to West End Avenue for a cab.

The taxi pulled up to the office building on Fifty-eighth Street as Gary Thorpe turned the corner. He saw Hardy and came over.

"Just the man I wanted to see. Ralph and I have a new book coming out, and we're having a party Friday night, why don't you come?"

"Sure," said Hardy. "What's the name of the book?"

"*The Nights are Short in Sweden* . . . I know, very esoteric title, but it has a lot of sex so we'll probably do all right. Bring Denise along to the party if you like."

Hardy chuckled at Thorpe's transparency. "Okay, Gary, I'll bring her."

"Good. Friday night, any time after eight. It's very

downtown in the SoHo section near Houston Street."
He took out a pen and a notebook. "Here's the address. A friend of mine is letting me use his art gallery. Don't forget to bring Denise. See you, Pat."

"Hey, wait a minute. You nearly drove it out of my head. I was coming to see you. How well do you know James Norse?"

"So-so. He'll be at the party Friday. What about him?"

"Never mind," said Hardy, "it wasn't important. See you."

"That's it? You came to see me just to ask me that?"

"That's it," said Hardy.

"And they say writers are crazy. See you Friday, and don't forget . . ."

"I'll bring Denise. There's one thing I have to say for you, Gary, you are subtle."

"Thanks . . . I think. Okay. Got to run."

His mission accomplished, Hardy bought a paper and a new *TV Guide* and returned home. The phone was ringing as he came in.

"Shut up, Holmes, I hear it. Hello."

It was Denise. She had gotten the commercial and it was a rush job. "So I'll be shooting all day tomorrow."

"Great," he said. "That'll give you all day Friday to rest up."

"For what?" she said archly.

"Get your mind out of bed. Gary Thorpe is having a big party and he invited me . . . and you. Do you want to go?"

"Okay," she said emphatically. "Oh, what a wonderful week this has turned out to be! And my week started last Friday."

"Thanks for the compliment. I think you're kind of cute, too. See you Friday. I'll pick you up about six and we can have dinner first."

"Let me cook for you," she said, "and come at five so we have time for coffee and things like that."

"I like the sound of 'things like that,'" he said.

"I knew you would. Friday. Bye."

Satisfied that there was nothing to be done until the party, Hardy called Laura and told her not to bother to come in on Thursday.

"All right," the housekeeper said with some exasperation. "I'll be there on Friday."

"Don't bother, Laura, let it go till next week. I'll pay you, of course."

"Patrick Anthony Hardy, I've known you since you were a little boy, so don't insult me by making it out to be just a matter of money. If your father were still alive, he'd pull down your pants and give you a good wallop on your behind."

Hardy was sorry he had started the whole thing. "Yes, Laura."

She had only paused just enough to take a breath. "By next Thursday the place will be a total mess. As it is, I'm only there long enough to give it a lick and a promise. I never saw such a man for privacy, except of course, your father. You're your father's son, all right."

"See you next week, Laura."

"If I live till then."

He hung up, breathed a sigh of relief and then checked to see if all the locks were secured. That done, he looked up the week's movie schedule and settled in for escape from the rest of the world.

On Thursday he grew tired of TV and pounced on some favorite books. By early Friday morning he had reread *Justine, The Outsider, The Glass Key* and all of *Sherlock Holmes.*

He read the last page of "The Adventure of the Retired Colourman" with the image of Basil Rathbone and the sound of the actor's voice pervading his mind. Hardy rubbed his eyes contentedly and yawned his way into the kitchen where he drank half a quart of orange juice. A short visit to the toilet, and he was back in bed and fast asleep.

He awoke at three, exercised, showered and shaved and leisurely sat around until it was time to go downtown.

At five minutes after five he knocked at Denise's door.

He heard her desperate response and then the door opened. Hardy squinted his eyes at the smoke.

"My lamb chops," she wailed.

After rescuing the lamb chops and salting out the fire, he poured them both a glass of wine.

As they started to drink, they both noticed a new burning smell. "The rice." This time she rushed into the kitchen.

The pizza arrived quick and hot. When they had finished and the box and string were cleared away and more wine poured and new cigarettes lit, it was only six-thirty.

"And I wanted to impress you with my culinary aptitude."

"You should see some of the disasters I've had in my kitchen," said Hardy as he glanced at his watch. "It's too early to go to the party."

She wrinkled up her nose. "Just what I was thinking."

Later as they cuddled together she said, "Do you really want to go to that party?"

"No. But I should. Come to think of it, my ambitious little actress, so should you. Gary Thorpe is interested. It could mean a role in his new movie."

"Or a roll in his old bed."

"Funny. Come on, get dressed."

"Aren't you the least bit jealous of Gary Thorpe?"

"You know I am. But you're your own person. Whatever you do is your own business."

She stood up in the bed. "All right, let me see if I have the ground rules straight. We go together, but we don't necessarily leave together."

"I didn't say that," he protested.

"No, but you meant it."

He was laughing. "I'm sorry, but nobody should have a temper tantrum when they're nude. It just doesn't make it."

"I am not having a temper tantrum."

"Okay, but you are nude, get dressed."

"Okay," and she flounced into the bathroom.

They decided to walk.

"You still mad?" asked Hardy.

"A little."

"Good. Knowing you, in a little while you won't be mad at all."

She smirked and pinched his hand. "You bastard."

"Ow, that hurt."

"Good." And she held him closer as they strolled.

Lower Broadway was very dark, very vast, very quiet and very lonely. The only sound they heard was their own footsteps.

Denise looked about warily. "Some place for a party."

He pointed his walking stick in front of them. " 'Into the valley of death rode the six hundred.' "

"Not funny."

Soon they noticed trickles of pedestrians and cars heading for a common destination. Hardy checked the address and in they went. A handwritten sign announced that the Thorpe/Price party was on the first floor. The music grew louder as they climbed the steep old-fashioned steps to the first floor where a busty blonde with a German accent and a low-cut dress greeted them. "Hello, I'm Elsa."

They told their names.

The blonde then recited, "The bar is back there, put your coats on the table next to it. Food is next to the bar. Dancing in the second room."

They thanked Elsa, and as they threaded their way in, they could hear her starting her litany again.

He considered the problems of retrieving their coats later from the collection on the table. He found a stack of unused frames in a corner and folded his trench coat and Denise's cape and stashed them there.

Denise was waiting for him at the bar with two clear plastic glasses of scotch. "Let's look around, okay?"

"Okay."

Beyond the coat table and the unused frames they discovered two sleeping alcoves behind curtains, decorated like harem rooms and complete with reostat lighting.

"Wall-to-wall mattress," said Hardy.

"If we get bored, we know where to go."

Ahead of them was a brick wall. They reversed their steps. Passing the bar area, he sniffed the air and she nodded.

"Pot, pot everywhere and all I've got is drink."

"You're getting better. That's very clever." He stopped in front of a piece of white statuary. "Get a load of this."

He examined the sculpture of a large breast and then leaned over to read the name. "Ha. It's called 'The American Dream,'" but Denise was talking to Gary Thorpe.

"Hi, Pat. Great party. Come on, Denise, there's a juke box in the next room playing music just for us." And they were gone.

Hardy found a wall and leaned on it. He sipped his drink and looked around. He spotted James Victor Norse talking to Elsa. Combining business with pleasure, he made his way over to them.

"Deserted your post, I see."

"I quit," she answered. "Nobody was listening anyway."

Norse offered his hand. "I'm Jim Norse. We've met before, but I don't remember your name."

"Patrick Hardy."

Elsa waved to a form in the crowd. "Harry, when did you get back?" And she was off to get her answer.

Norse shook his head. "It seems we both dropped the ball."

Hardy watched as she moved away. "I never even got my hands on it."

They looked at each other in agreement and drank their drinks.

"Are you in show business, Mr. Hardy?"

"No. I'm a private detective."

"Really. I've never met a private detective before." His head moved as someone appeared at Hardy's shoulder. "Terry, there you are. Terry Hyde, Patrick Hardy. Mr. Hardy is a private detective."

The young man put on an amazed look. Hardy tensed up as he recognized the face. Automatically his eyes went to the young man's hands and all the glittering rings he wore.

"Terry, why don't you get us some fresh drinks. What are you drinking, Mr. Hardy?"

"Scotch."

"Right. Terry, we'll be sitting on the bench over by that picture made of balloons."

"Yes, Mr. Norse."

Terry Hyde brought their drinks, and the three indulged in inconsequential party conversation. Hardy didn't know what the game was, but he played it. In a short time Hyde drifted away, and soon after that so did Norse.

Hardy tried to figure out if something had happened and he had missed it. He gave it up as a lost cause when he saw Ralph Price. He hadn't done too well with Norse, maybe Price would be more profitable. Hardy was just starting toward him when the large man jostled his arm and spilled his drink.

"Don't worry about it," said Hardy. "My fault."

"You're damn right it was your fault."

The man's tone was familiar. It made Hardy's bowels queasy and his feet anxious to run. He smiled weakly. "Sorry."

"Screw you and sorry," said the big man and started a left hook toward Hardy's midsection.

Adrenaline exploded into Hardy's system pushing his fears aside. Using his walking stick as if he were bayonet fighting, he parried the left and in the same motion poked the stick at the man's neck. The big man was fast and sidestepped, throwing a right as he did. This left him wide open. Hardy slashed upward with the bottom of the stick, catching his opponent in the stomach. The man was stopped, but Hardy completed the maneuver with a butt stroke to the chest.

If the crowd hadn't pressed in, Hardy would have continued working on the fallen man. He stood shiv-

76

ering for a moment, then went to the bar for a shot of scotch and then into the toilet where he vomited.

When he was himself again and had washed up, he came back out to the party. The people there all acted as if nothing had happened. Hardy foraged around the food table, loading his plate with a little of everything. Back to the bar for a ginger ale, and then to a corner of the room where he could recuperate.

He looked up from his almost empty plate to see Elsa sitting next to him. "I saw what happened. I admire a man of action. How would you like to take me home?"

Hardy looked at those mammoth breasts and was tempted, but his better judgment made him consider. The man who started the fight could have been sicked on him by Norse and Hyde for whatever their reasons. Elsa could be another ploy. He had seen her talking to Norse. Regretfully he said no. She shrugged her shoulders, causing her breasts to almost leap out at him. He bemoaned his caution even as she stood up and left.

They were out of scotch. He settled for vodka and sipped it distastefully as he wandered among the dancers looking for Denise and Gary Thorpe. The two were nowhere to be seen. Neither was Ralph Price nor Norse nor Hyde. Hardy went back to the bar for another drink. This time he had to settle for red wine. On his return trip he was told the bar was closed.

Time to go home. Where was his coat? While he was remembering, a very thin cigarette was placed between his lips. He took grateful breaths of the marijuana and surveyed the woman who was holding it to his mouth. Not as busty as Elsa and a little older, but nice. Very nice.

"I'm Pat Hardy. What's your name?"

"Victoria Leonard, but you can call me Vickie."
Her breath smelled of pretzels. It was nice.

"Vickie," he said, putting one finger to his lips.
"You wait here."

Hardy took another drag and returned the joint to
his new found friend. He retrieved his coat, noticing
that Denny's cape was gone. He was in no mood to
peek behind the curtains of the sleeping alcoves.

"Voila, Vickie my love, I have returned."

"That's nice. I have a waterbed at home."

"Then let's go home and go to bed."

Chapter Nine

Unfortunately Vickie's waterbed had more bounce than she did. The minute she showed the bed to him, she fell across it and passed out.

Hardy was in no condition to venture out into the streets alone. He knew this and decided if nothing else, he would get a night's sleep. He undressed and rolled his hostess over to one side of the bed. As he did he got very hung up on her earrings. They appeared to be sharp things that would puncture the bed and drown them both. It seemed to take forever, but he undid the gold posts that secured the rings to her ears.

Rings. Everything that happened lately seemed to be about rings. The pierced holes in her ears excited him. Very Freudian, that. Now he was looking at the earrings. The gold posts seemed to be growing larger, till they looked like giant pillars. The seven pillars of wisdom. No, there were only two. The two pillows of wisdom. He buried his head in the pillows and slept, dreaming about wisdom. There were a lot of things he ought to know.

It was a very pleasant awakening. Vickie's manipulations had aroused him before they had awakened him. Awareness came to him just as they were coupling. He was too content to move, but she was more than making up for it . . . so was the waterbed. He hadn't found wisdom, but this would do.

The purple bathroom was very nice. He hadn't done too badly. There was even shaving gear which he took advantage of. She wasn't in the bedroom when he came out. The bed looked inviting, but he smelled bacon frying. He dressed quickly, smiling as he picked up his two-pound ankle bracelet from where he had neatly folded it the night before.

The cooking smells led him to a small breakfast nook where a fully dressed Victoria was waiting with a glass of juice in one hand and a cup of coffee in the other. "How do you like your eggs?"

"Scrambled soft."

She served his eggs and poured herself a cup of coffee. She seemed pleased by the way he was enjoying the breakfast.

When he was done she offered him another thin cigarette. He shook his head and lit up one of his own Marlboros. She refilled his coffee cup, kissed him on the brow, "You're nice," walked into the living room where she took her coat from the back of a chair and walked to the door. "Goodbye, Pat. You're very nice."

Hardy watched her action with a great deal of puzzlement and was about to ask what was happening when James Norse and Terry Hyde came in as she went out.

Despite the bind he was in and despite the enjoyable time Vickie had given him in bed that morning, the only thought in his mind in that immediate second was what he had missed by saying no to Elsa and those wonderful breasts.

The second was over now, and James Norse was speaking. "Good morning, Mr. Hardy, I hope you spent a comfortable night."

"Excuse me, Mr. Norse, but can't we skip this polite crap." That was Terry Hyde. "You're pretty cute with that stick, gimpy, want to try it on me?"

"Relax, Terry, there's plenty of time for that. First, we'll talk."

The expression "first we'll talk" sounded much too ominous to Hardy. Using his walking stick for leverage he literally dove for the bedroom praying there would be a lock on the door. There was. He snapped it shut and tried not to notice the shock waves coming from his knee as he looked for a way out. Hyde was yelling and Norse was cajoling and either or both were hammering at the door.

The windows were locked, and there was no fire escape. He broke one of the panes with his stick and leaned out and yelled. The street was deserted and even if it wasn't, who would listen.

The door to the bedroom was starting to give. Hardy looked about frantically. For some reason he thought of earrings. The next thought was, puncture the bed. Using his trench coat to protect his hands, he picked up a shard of glass and started to hack away at the bed. The glass broke. Using the remainder, he kept at it.

They were almost through the door.

"I'll break your other leg, you gimp bastard."

"Don't be a fool, Mr. Hardy, you're only managing to annoy me more . . ."

At this juncture the door burst open . . . and so

did the bed. The two men came in and the water went out. Hardy felt the cascade pushing him along. Taking advantage of the confusion, he threw his coat over Norse's head and clouted Hyde in the shins with his stick. Pushing Norse into Hyde, he hopped toward the outside door. There were two locks. He turned them both and pulled the knob. The door wouldn't budge, obviously one lock had been closed and the other open, he had only reversed them.

Hardy looked back to see that the two men were on the floor and still dealing with the water.

They would be up soon.

He grabbed at one of the locks and turned and pulled the door knob. Nothing. Now he turned both locks and tried again. The door opened and he nearly fell in his frenetic effort to get out.

Lots of stairs. He stumbled down them like a three-legged horse. The pain in his leg combined with the fear in his gut and the clammy cold wetness of his clothing and sent one major distress signal to his brain.

As he ran out to the street, the lower half of him sopping wet, he had the weirdest feeling, as if he had been there before. It was true. Last night he had been too stoned to notice but that was Kate's building opposite and he had been in the building across the street all night.

He could hear them on the stairs.

Missed opportunities of investigation and fear of his pursuers tangled and boggled his mind. They were right behind him. Which way? The Drive? The Park? Broadway?

No time. Any direction and they would see him and catch him. Hardy didn't feel like taking that conjecture any further. His leg ached. The two-pound weight felt like twenty. The street was empty.

Hardy ran across to Kate's building. Wait in the hall? He was soaking wet and freezing. The Pritchetts? No.

He clumped upstairs to Ronald Fried's apartment. Desperate, he raised his hand to hammer on the door, but caution changed the hammering to a tapping.

"Hello," the voice called from inside. Thank God he was home.

"It's me, Pat Hardy."

"Just a minute," the voice crooned.

Even in his fear Hardy was aware of the change of tone in Ron Fried's voice.

"My, what are you doing up so early on a Saturday morning?"

"No time to talk, Ronny, just let me in and keep quiet."

"I'm flattered that you've come to see me, but you don't have to be so rude . . . is it raining? Look at you, you're soaking wet, and no coat on a day like this. You better get out of those wet things before you catch your death."

Again thoughts mingled. The word death reminded him of what was outside. Now he was fairly safe, but he had Ronny to contend with. And, he had lost his new trench coat.

Hardy went to the window to peek. Ronny joined him there.

"Get back," hissed Hardy, and he watched Norse and Hyde standing and talking and gesturing and looking.

"Ronny," he shivered, "you wouldn't have a pair of pants I could borrow, would you? And a towel too, please."

"Coming right up."

Hardy leaned against the warm radiator cover and continued to watch the two men. Hyde nodded and ran around the corner while Norse paced impatiently.

Ronny came back with a whiskey, a towel and a pair of pants. Hardy gulped the drink, welcoming the heat it brought.

"Thanks."

He thought about going into the bathroom to change, mentally laughed it off as unsophisticated and dropped his soggy pants to the floor. He wanted to remove his wet shorts too, but his sophistication didn't go that far. He wiped himself with the towel and continued his vigil of the street. Hyde had brought the limousine around and Norse was getting in. Hardy breathed a sigh of relief as they drove off.

"Would you mind telling me what this is all about?" Ronny asked.

Hardy didn't have a chance to answer. Someone knocked on and simultaneously opened the apartment door. The someone was Ted McLean. He saw Ronny near Hardy, who had his pants draped around his feet, and said, "Sorry, I didn't know you were entertaining."

Ronny rolled his eyes and threw up his hands dramatically. "Teddy, don't be such a bitch. It's not at all what you think."

"It never is."

Hardy didn't say a word. He just stood there, visualizing the painting of September Morn, but with his face.

"I'm Ted McLean."

"Pat Hardy, we've met before."

"Really, I don't remember."

Hardy hiked up his pants.

84

Silence.

Hardy was annoyed, embarrassed and cold. "Ronny, would you tell me where the bathroom is so I can get out of these things and warm up."

"Of course, and don't mind Ted. That's just his way."

In the bathroom he wrapped his wet shorts in his wet pants, dried himself again and put on the pants Ronny had given him. They were a trifle tight, but he had no other choice. He ignored his wet feet. What he wanted to do was leave immediately, but he was still too cold to face the weather, besides Norse and Hyde might be cruising the neighborhood. Like it or not, this was the best place for him.

He put his shoes back on over his wet socks and went out and told the two essentially what had happened but changed Norse into a jealous husband.

They accepted the story, but McLean kept glaring at Fried, and Fried pretended to cast admiring glances at Hardy. At least Hardy hoped they were a pretense.

Fried noticed the lump of clothes Hardy was holding.

"Why don't you let me hang those up for you? They'll never dry that way."

"No thanks. I have to be going soon anyway."

"Oh, do you have to?" said McLean caustically.

"Ronny, thanks for everything. You really got me out of a jam and I appreciate it. I'll bring your pants back."

"No hurry," said Ronny, and he smiled at Hardy and then at McLean.

The tense atmosphere was getting on Hardy's nerves. When he felt warm enough, he went to the window to check whether or not Norse and Hyde had returned. They had not.

"Thanks again, Ronny. Ted, nice meeting you. Goodbye." He picked up his stick, and clutching his wet bundle to him, he fled.

On the Drive he saw a bus coming. He rushed to the bus stop as best he could with his bad leg and his tight pants and the two-pound weight on his ankle. While he moved, he mind chose to dwell on the weight strapped to his foot. Had they seen it? What did they think of it? Did they think he was weird for wearing it?

His self-examination ceased while he got on the bus. Of course there was no money in the pants he had on.

Hardy unrolled his wet bundle just enough to find change for the toll box, then he sat down and looked out the window for the rest of the trip, avoiding the staring eyes of the other passengers.

At home he dropped the wet clothes in a corner, took several tranquilizers and a hot bath and went to bed.

His growling stomach woke him. It was still daytime. He washed his face and gargled and wandered into the kitchen. He was hungry but didn't know what he wanted to eat. He closed the frig door empty-handed and opened a cupboard where he found some wheat thins for himself and a biscuit for Holmes. When the box was empty, he went back to the refrigerator for an orange. While he peeled he knew he should tell Friday what had happened.

He couldn't prove anything, but perhaps the cops could use the information. He popped a section of orange in his mouth and dialed Manhattan North. Friday was off that day. Hardy finished the orange and after looking up Friday's home phone, he called it.

"Jesus Christ, Pat, it's my day off."

"Sorry to bother you, but I . . . Never mind I'll be in touch at your office on Monday."

"As long as you called," said Friday, "tell me now."

He related his experiences of the night before and this morning, leaving out the part about Fried and McLean.

"Okay, very interesting. You going to make a complaint?"

"No," said Hardy, "I couldn't prove a thing. Norse and Hyde would alibi each other and where would that leave me? It did occur to me that Norse has, or should I say had, some sort of illegal thing going on in that house. If you decide to get a warrant and check it out, it'll probably be as innocent as a church by now. But if by living across the street, Kate or Dave Bishop knew what was going on in that building, it could have been a reason for killing them. Something must have been going on there otherwise why would Hyde have jumped me when I first started nosing around?"

"What are you talking about?"

Hardy told the policemen about his first meeting with Hyde in the alley.

"Why the hell didn't you mention this before?"

"It didn't seem important."

"Is that all?" Friday asked impatiently.

"No. One more idea. It might be interesting to ask your computer what type blood James Norse has. He could be that unknown man you were looking for. The one who was taking care of her and buying all those clothes. It's just a wild thought."

"Thanks. But from now on keep your wild

thoughts to days when I'm on duty . . . if I learn anything I'll let you know. Goodbye."

Hardy hung up, finished the orange and revisited the refrigerator. This time he made a sliced onion sandwich, salting it a lot more than was good for him.

There was a movie on TV in an hour. He got dressed and leashed up Holmes and walked over to Broadway. It was too early for the complete *Times* and *News* so he took the Magazine and Theatre and Comic sections along with a copy of *Penthouse*. From there he went to Zabar's. There were only ten people ahead of him at the delicacy counter of the grocery so he decided to wait. When he left he was loaded with Nova Scotia and herring and white fish. One more stop at the bagel place and then home they went.

Things were put away, Holmes' ground chuck was out of the freezer and thawing and Hardy was in front of the TV with a large drink. The phone rang.

It was Denise.

"Yeah, Denise. What is it?"

"I'm sorry."

"Okay, fine. Goodbye."

"I mean, I'm really sorry."

"Okay. We both agreed how it would be. You felt like splitting with Thorpe and you did."

"It wasn't like that, Pat. He wanted to show me his script."

He wanted to laugh but he couldn't. Denise kept talking. "He's really a very sweet man. He really showed me the script. We spent the whole night reading it and he's going to give me a part in the picture."

"That's fine. I hope it's your big break."

"Pat, could I come over?"

"Why?"

"Because I'm sorry, and I miss you, and I'm lonely, and I miss you."

He closed his eyes and rubbed his nose. He didn't relish spending the night alone either. "Sure, Denny, come ahead."

When she did, they made love and watched television and ate herring and bagels for supper and Nova Scotia salmon and eggs and bagels for breakfast and white fish and bagels for lunch. Sunday afternoon the two of them and Holmes walked around Riverside Park. If Hyde or any other of Norse's men was following them, Hardy didn't want to know about it. Tomorrow would be soon enough to think about those things, if at all.

She was still there Monday morning when the phone rang. She stirred but slept on. He answered it.

It was Gerald Friday. "Good morning. I hope I woke you."

"What's up?"

"After I spoke to you I started wondering about that house. Do you know what it's like to get the proper papers on a weekend to enter and search a house? Well, if there was anything there, it's gone now. Deserted. Not even the waterbed."

"Who owns the building?

"A corporation."

"And . . . ?"

"What did you expect? It's a dummy corporation with a vacant lot for an address."

Hardy started to light a cigarette but changed his mind. "I bet if you dig a little deeper you find that that corporation is a dummy set up under the financial umbrella of James Victor Norse."

"You're probably right," said Friday, "but I've already stuck my neck out too far as it is. I hope nobody ever asks me why I checked that place out in the first place."

"Tell them you got a tip from an informant."

"Thanks a lot. Tell me one thing, Private Detective, is there a woman in your bed right now?"

"Yes."

"Do you plan to stay in that bed with her all morning?"

"Yes."

"I'll be a son of a bitch! With you it is just like the paperbacks. You'll excuse me, won't you?" he said sarcastically. "I've got a lot of reports to fill out and a lot of boring routine work to do, and a lot more cases than you'll ever see in a lifetime. And when I think of you in that bed and me here . . ."

He didn't finish the sentence.

"Yes," said Hardy.

"Go to hell, Private Detective."

He smiled as he hung up the phone and woke Denise in the nicest way he knew how.

Chapter Ten

Denise had gone home and Hardy was still in bed. The TV was on. Since there were no movies, he was watching *Boxes*, a game show in which celebrities played against each other, and the winner's prize went to a member of the audience. Hardy didn't really care for the show, but one of this week's guests was the actress Susannah Dow. Another Hollywood beauty had once said that Susannah Dow made her feel like a boy. It was precisely for that reason that Hardy was watching.

When the show was over he got out of bed, had a salami sandwich on Armenian bread and went about making boeuf a la Catalane for that evening's supper.

While the bacon was simmering in water, he dried the chunks of beef and browned them. Then he fried the bacon slightly along with the sliced onions. He placed the three ingredients in a casserole and cooked a cup of rice in the frying pan for about three minutes. Three hours and bouillon and tomatoes and spices and a movie and a half later, he set the casserole aside to cool.

Most cooks skimmed the fat at this point. Hardy being Hardy, waited till it cooled and then put it in the refrigerator. Later he would remove the coagulated fat and then add the rice, and cook it all for another twenty-five minutes.

He loaded the dishwasher, sneezing from the soap, and set a load to washing while he sat at his desk and tried to set his mind to thinking.

His hands smelled from the garlic. He went into the bathroom and rubbed Brut into them. Not satisfied with the effect, he washed his hands. Now he went back to his desk.

Frustrated at not being able to think of anything, he jumped up and dressed and left the apartment, much to Holmes's distress. Despite the day's preparations, Hardy decided to have dinner in the same restaurant he had taken Denise. It wasn't that he preferred Nero's food to his, but the last visit had made things happen. Maybe it would again.

As the cab rolled downtown and he remembered the happenings in the "house across the street" with Norse and Hyde, he wondered if he shouldn't forget the whole cockeyed scheme and go back home and eat his beef stew with rice.

He was there.

Reluctantly he got out and climbed the stairs to the steakhouse.

Susannah Dow.

Gary Thorpe was having dinner with Susannah Dow. All thoughts of the case went out the window. Hardy's only concern was meeting Susannah Dow and perhaps doing to Gary what he was sure Gary had done to him with Denise by doing the same to Susannah Dow. He cleared his mind of the jumbled syntax his lechery had produced and marched directly to their table.

"Gary. Great to see you again. Oh, I'm sorry, didn't mean to intrude." And he stopped talking and stood there.

Gary Thorpe tried to wait him out, but couldn't cut it.

"Susannah Dow, Patrick Hardy. Pat, Sue."

The actress who was quite aware that the two men were dueling didn't bother to hide her amusement and in fact encouraged the competition.

"Would you care to join us . . . Pat?"

"I wouldn't dream . . ."

"No. He wouldn't dream," Gary said emphatically.

"Then on the other hand, I'd only kick myself later for letting phony manners get in the way of accepting a gracious invitation from Susannah Dow. I accept."

And Hardy was sitting and motioning to the waiter.

He ate and drank with great gusto and was thoroughly charming to Sue and equally obnoxious to Gary . . . and when the check came, he blatantly let Thorpe pay it.

To Thorpe's discomfort Hardy was still with them as they received their coats from the checkroom girl and were on their way out.

"Hardy."

He looked around to see Ralph Price glaring at him.

"Hi," said Hardy and was ready to turn back to his two dinner companions when he felt Price's strong hand firmly gripping his forearm.

This was one of the problems Hardy's Army training had never quite solved. When left to his own devices and options, Hardy always ran like the coward he was. When definitely attacked, his brain hid and his reflexes took over, and despite his reluctance, he became a very efficient combatant. But, when faced with a circumstance that was neither here nor there, neither was Hardy. This was just one of those situations.

"Let go," Hardy said, his voice going up half an octave, and he almost broke Price's thumb. "I'm sorry. I'm sorry. I'm sorry," he said.

Price's cry of pain had brought the maitre d' over. "Is anything wrong, Mr. Price?"

"It's nothing," said Hardy. "It's all right."

Price added his assent with a nod and the maitre d' bent over and retrieved Hardy's walking stick, handed it to him and left.

"I'm sorry. I didn't mean to do that. I just don't like anyone to get physical with me. Look, do you mind if we get a drink."

They went to the bar where Hardy ordered two scotches. When he finished his, he apologized again.

"All right, forget it," said Price, "but next time you start something like that, I'll be the one to finish it."

Hardy wanted to tell him that it wasn't he who had started it, but thought better of it. He looked around but Gary and Sue had gone. Price had run interference very well for his partner.

Price tasted his drink and tried not to rub or look at his thumb. "What the hell do you want?"

"What do you mean?" said Hardy.

"Don't play games. Ever since that first day in our office you've been under our noses like some ugly fungus."

Hardy signaled for two more drinks. "Ugly fungus.

Sounds good, but I don't really think what you just said means anything. Or do all writers do that?"

"I said no more games. What do you want?"

Suddenly Hardy felt very tired. "I want to find out who killed Kate Arnheim."

Hardy wasn't sure but he thought he sensed a spasm of pain going through the writer and that it wasn't from his thumb. Whatever it was, it was gone now.

His mask back up, Price said, "And you think I don't? Or do you think I killed her?"

"I don't know what I think any more," the detective answered, "but maybe if I get a few straight answers it would help."

"Such as?"

"Were you in love with Kate?"

"None of your damned business . . ."

Hardy sat down on a bar stool. The writer looked at their reflections in the mirror. "Yes I was."

Hardy lit a cigarette. "Don't take this except as a basis for a question. I mean, I cared for her, too . . . Kate slept around a lot. Were you jealous? Did you fight about it?"

"Yes, two times." Price's face was wooden.

"About anyone in particular?"

"No."

"Where were you Christmas Eve?"

"I've told the cops that. Home, and alone."

"Not much of an alibi."

"It's the only one I've got. Now if you don't mind, good night."

"One more thing. What's the connection between you and James Norse?"

"That's also none of your business, but if it will get you off my back . . . he's thinking about going into movies, and if we come up with a picture he likes, he might produce it. Good night."

Hardy sat there and rubbed his knee. It had begun to ache. The fact of the ache made him look down. Sitting on a bar stool is no extraordinary feat, but it is something of an accomplishment to someone who has been dragging around a stiff leg for a time. Hardy smiled. His left knee was bent almost as much as his right. He bent it a little more and stopped smiling. That really hurt. He finished off his drink, paid the tab and spent the entire cab ride home worrying if he had injured his knee in any way by bending it more than he should. He fought the impulse to call either of his doctors, soaked the pain away in a hot tub and went to bed.

He couldn't sleep. He didn't want to take a tranquilizer. He'd been using them too often lately.

He got out of bed and limped to the fireplace. He limped more than he had to, and realizing that he was playacting for himself, he stopped and walked in as normal a manner as he could.

The thought of lighting a fire came into his mind along with images of himself as Basil Rathbone cum Sherlock Holmes, basking in front of it and figuring out the case.

Too much work to light the fire. He dismissed the thought along with the fantasy and went instead to the small bookcase beneath the window.

The Confessions of St. Augustine was a good choice. Hardy was asleep within fifteen minutes.

Tuesday morning. Part of his mind told him it would be a good day to stay in bed, another part sent him the message that his bladder needed emptying. The bladder won.

He tried to get back to sleep, but now that he was up he was hungry.

"All right, Holmes, get up. If I don't sleep, nobody sleeps."

The dog opened one eye disdainfully and closed it again.

Hardy invented many reasons for not going into the gym, but none of them were acceptable, even to himself.

It was a good workout and the knee was coming along very well. He sang as he showered and shaved and planned breakfast.

When he started for the kitchen, Holmes was up and right behind him. "Where the hell do you think you're going?"

The poodle barked a happy response and wagged his tail.

After a ham and potato omelet of which Holmes got a share, they went out for the paper and the mail and a morning walk. It was only when they were back inside that Hardy realized he had worn the weight and hadn't taken the walking stick.

Very pleased with himself, he went to his desk and sorted out the mail. Bills and a card from Steve Macker. Nothing from Ruby. Hardy spent several seconds considering how and why he missed her and then settled down to work.

He was ready. The trouble was he was also stuck. He took the material from the cork wall and read it through. When he pinned it back up, his only ideas were to revisit the Pritchetts or to call Kate's mother in California.

He picked up the phone and called Denise instead. She wasn't in. He left word with her service and called Manhattan North. Friday gave him Kate's mother's new address in San Francisco.

"A couple of more things," said the policeman, "James Victor Norse is blood type B."

"For Christ's sake, does everybody in America have type B?"

"Nope. Terry Hyde doesn't."

"What else can you tell me about him?" said Hardy swiveling in his chair and pinning the Bowers' new address to the cork wall.

"Not too much. No priors. Been arrested, but never convicted. Comes from Milwaukee originally. Got out of the Marines a couple of years ago. Honorable discharge. No combat. Thought of as a pretty tough person. All we know for sure is that he's Norse's chauffeur and bodyguard . . . and man of odd jobs."

"Such as?" asked Hardy.

"You name it. Another thing, you have to wade through three different companies to get to it, but Norse owns that building."

As he sometimes did, Friday hung up the phone without bothering to say goodbye. Hardy got a dial tone and called the operator. She told him to dial 415-555-1212 for San Francisco information. He pushed down the receiver ready to do just that when the phone rang.

"May I speak to Patrick Hardy, please."

The sound of her voice was an immediate turn-on. "Good morning, Sue, it's me."

Susannah Dow made a purring noise. "You recognized my voice. That's very flattering."

Hardy made an inane response.

"You could do me a wonderful favor. Peter was supposed to fly in from London today, but they've extended the conference and he won't be able to make it."

It took Hardy a second or two to realize she was speaking about her husband, Peter Craig, who was some sort of important person in government. She was still talking. "I have these tickets for the O'Neill revival and I was wondering if you would be a darling and be my escort."

He didn't stop to think why she had called him. He didn't care. "Yes, I'd be delighted."

"That's simply marvelous."

Hardy took a deep breath and said, "I have a great idea. I happen to be a very good cook. Would you consider having drinks and dinner here with me before we go?"

"What a charming way to put it. 'Would I consider.' You really are a gentleman of the old school. I would adore it. I'll be there between four thirty and five. That way we won't have to rush. I hate rushing through anything."

"Seven Riverside Drive. Don't go around the corner to the main building. I have my own private entrance right on the Drive."

"How charming. Till later, then."

He sat there in shock. Then he looked about at the messy apartment. Of all times not to have had Laura come. He scrambled around grabbing up strewn-about clothing and shoes and flinging them into closets. He turned on the tub for a bath.

"At least dinner won't be too big a problem," he muttered to himself as he took the boeuf a la Catalane out of the refrigerator and picked out the slivers of white fat that had surfaced. He placed the casserole and cup of rice on the butcher's table.

"Shut up, Holmes," and realized why the animal was barking.

He raced into the bathroom and shut off the mounting water just in time. As he walked back to the kitchen he stopped to dust the table tops with his handkerchief. On his short cleaning trip he enjoyed the realization that the brief run hadn't bothered his leg at all.

In this multifaceted good mood he continued getting the apartment, dinner and himself ready for Susannah Dow.

Chapter Eleven

He couldn't believe it. She was there. In his apartment, sitting on his couch, petting his dog.

A confused thought about petting and other things glanced off his brain.

"What's your pleasure?"

"That, Pat, is a very leading question. Is that a Beckman?" she asked pointing to an etching hanging on the wall.

"Yes, 'Cafe Musik.' "

"I thought I recognized it." She looked about the room. "You have very good taste."

"Thank you, Ma'am."

"You 'Ma'am' me again and I'll kick your ass. Where's my drink?"

"What'll it be?"

"Martini, very dry."

"Vodka or gin?"

"Vodka, darling, definitely vodka."

He couldn't keep his eyes away from her breasts. She noticed and laughed. "Hey, I have a face, too."

"Sorry," he laughed back. "They were starting to hypnotize me."

"Remarks like that will get you everywhere. Where's my drink?"

"Are you a fanatic about how dry your martini is?"

"Yes. After you get to know me a little better, you'll find out that I'm a fanatic about almost everything I do."

He watched as she unwound from the couch. "Show me the mixings and I'll make them."

"I can't wait for the part where you shake them."

"You're out of luck, my dear, you don't shake martinis, you stir them, gently, so as not to bruise any part thereof. You amaze me. A grown man not knowing that."

"It slipped my mind. I seemed to have other things on it," he leered.

She shook her head and leered back, making a comic face out of it.

He got embarrassed for no reason in particular and sputtered, "I don't usually drink martinis."

"Oh, what a disappointment. I wanted to share my secret formula with you. Say you'll have a martini with me."

"Okay."

"I mean really say it. 'I'd love to have a martini with you.'"

He hated martinis with a passion. "I'd love to have a martini with you."

"Thank you." She handed him his drink. "See how simple it is to please me." She flashed that sexy look she was famous for and went back to the couch and patted it with her hand in an invitation for him to join her.

She sipped, and looked at him, waiting for him to

follow suit. He did and suppressed the face the bad taste in his mouth wanted him to make.

"Isn't that super, darling?"

He smiled and breathed in all her odors. "Super."

She thought the boeuf a la Catalane was super, too. As was the Cockburn's port and the coffee and Cointreau.

Hardy was having a hard time keeping up with her. The port and the brandy hadn't bothered him, but the martinis . . .

". . . Peter and I see each other so seldom. Now that I'm a big star and he's a big wheel for Uncle Sam. It's a very lonely life at the top."

He didn't notice her maudlin tone. He was more concerned with the fight going on within himself between his sex drive and his aversion to vodka and vermouth.

She was sitting on the couch again, and he was in the wing chair by the window.

"Why are you always so far away from me? Come here."

As he moved to comply, she adjusted a pillow on the couch and found the *TV Guide* where he had stuffed it earlier in his hasty attempt to clean up.

"Hey," she said, "I think someone told me that one of my movies is on." She thumbed through the magazine. "Here it is. *Cave Woman*. The first picture I ever did. It's real stinker but my bod really looks great. Where's the TV?"

Hardy folded back the louver doors that hid the living room television set and turned it on. He glanced at his watch but said nothing.

Sue had kicked off her shoes and had her legs tucked under her. "Come on, watch with me."

He joined her on the couch.

"There she is," the actress exclaimed. "Look at that chest."

"That's what I've been doing all evening."

"On the screen, on the screen." And she clutched his leg as the younger edition of herself grunted and posed in a scant cave girl costume.

"Look at those boobs," she said and she was caressing the designated area. "And those legs." She had removed her hand from his thigh and was rubbing her own.

This went on for several minutes until the screen cave man kissed the screen cave girl. Susannah imitated her movie self with Hardy. The woman's ferocity surprised him. She bit him on the neck. He remembered that she had once made a vampire movie and was glad they weren't watching that.

He reached to undo her clothes.

"No."

He wasn't sure what that "no" meant. She explained.

"Love me. Make love to me. I need to be loved . . . but we can't get undressed. We have to go to the theatre."

All the time she talked she was adjusting her clothes and then his so that what she wanted could be affected.

She sighed as he put his face between those magnificent mounds of flesh. All that clothing made him feel like a teenager in a car. He moved his face from her bosom to kiss her.

"Don't smear my makeup."

Hardy settled for hanging onto those well-publicized breasts and resting his head on her shoulder and just going at it.

She went at it, too.

The woman was like a raging bull, or should that be cow? A portion of his mind conjectured over the metaphor as the mental process gave way to one a little more basic.

He was content to lie there and enjoy the afterglow with his head resting on her breast. She picked up his wrist and checked his watch. "Time to freshen up and go, my dear." She stood up. "I simply adore these new materials. Look, barely a wrinkle. Where's the bathroom? Come on, darling, don't dawdle. We just have time to make the curtain, and I'm crazy about O'Neill."

The play was a bore and he had a headache. And to top it all off, he was still horny. Afterward, he thought. But he was sorely disappointed.

In the lobby of her hotel she said loudly, "Good night. Thank you so much." Then she gave him a sisterly peck on the cheek and whispered, "Call me." And before he knew it she was in the elevator and gone.

His bed rocked like the Titanic going down for the last time, but he finally managed to get to sleep.

He dreamed about cave men pounding on his head with clubs. They looked like Norse and Hyde and Fried and Friday and Thorpe and Price. And through it all he could hear Kate Arnheim saying, "Dear Jesus, somebody please help me," while Susannah Dow was saying, "Don't smear my makeup."

When he awoke he was sick, very sick, and all the aspirin and orange juice didn't help a bit. Holmes tagged after him with a mournful look in his eyes as if to say, "I wish I could help."

He had managed to drift off to sleep again when the phone jangled him back.

"Hardy, it's me, Friday."

"Hurray."

"Save your sarcasm. I'm only calling so you'll get off my back about the Kate Arnheim case. We got the guy."

"What?"

"He did it again last night. Same m.o. First he raped her and then he slashed her to ribbons. This time people heard the victim's screams and called the cops. They caught the kid in the street. When he got to the station he confessed to doing the Arnheim girl, too."

"Come on, Friday. It's almost March. Kate was killed in December. There's a big gap there that just doesn't follow."

"It does if he's been in jail all this time, waiting trial on another charge . . . and his blood type is B."

Hardy groaned. "Where did it happen?" he asked.

"Lower East Side. Madison Street. Spanish kid, Carlos Ortega," said Friday.

He still felt sick and it was making him mean. Spitefully he said, "Tell me one thing, Friday, aren't you glad he was a Puerto Rican and not a black kid?" He hung up the phone.

As an afterthrough Hardy took the phone off the hook and shoved it under the pillow. Then he crawled to the other side of the bed and forced himself back to sleep. As he did he found himself wondering if he had ever met a woman kinkier than Susannah Dow, and he thought about the Duchess and dreamt about her.

Her monocle was twinkling and her body was writhing and her violet nails were clawing at him and as they made love in his dream she was saying, "You're being stupid. You're overlooking something. You're being stupid."

And Kate was saying, "Dear Jesus, somebody help

me," and Susannah Dow was saying, "Don't smear my makeup," and Friday was saying, "A black man made it with your girl." And Denny was saying, "You're so gentle. I love being made love to by a gentle man."

"You're a gentleman of the old school," Sue was saying, but it wasn't Sue, it was Ronny in drag. And Ted McLean had joined the crowd of cave men who were pounding away at his head. And Holmes was barking.

And Hardy woke up.

His dream had been so upsetting that he had thrown himself out of bed. The activity had thrown Holmes out of the same bed and the startled animal who hated violence as much as his owner did, was barking in anger and terror.

Partly to relieve the poodle and partly to relieve his own aching head, Hardy petted the dog until he had calmed down and stopped barking.

The phone rang and Holmes started barking again.

"Holmes! Hello."

"Mr. Hardy, my name is Zola Lieberman. We've never met, but I'm your neighbor in 14 . . ."

He cut her off. "Excuse me, Miss Lieberman, I hate to . . ."

"Mrs."

"Excuse me, Mrs. Lieberman, but may I ask what this call is all about?"

"Well, there is a question among some of the tenants whether or not the building should go co-op. We were wondering if you would care to join us in a meeting to . . ."

"Thank you, Mrs. Lieberman, but no thank you."

"I assure you that it will be to your best interests to attend."

"I'm sure you're right," he said, "but I can't make it. Goodbye."

What now?

They had caught Kate's killer and whoever had shot David Bishop was the city's problem. Hardy's problem was threefold: his hangover, staying forever out of James Victor Norse and Terry Hyde's way, and doing some work to bring money in.

He showered and got dressed. Masochistically, he strapped the weight to his leg, then he and Holmes walked slowly over to Broadway for a newspaper. It was all there, the Spanish kid's picture, the victim's picture and in a small insert in the corner, Kate's picture.

He threw the paper away and they went and spent a little time in the park.

Later while Holmes wolfed down his ground chuck and Hardy forced himself to eat a plateful of cottage cheese, they heard about it again on the news.

He got up and turned off the radio and turned on the television to a rerun of *Mission Impossible*.

He was tired and his back ached and . . . he remembered a favorite expression of his father's. "Don't get your bowels in an uproar," the old man used to say. Well, that was exactly where they were at this moment.

Hardy turned off the TV and tried to read. No go. He ran himself a bath and sat in the barber chair to decide whether to take the bath or not. Holmes sat at his feet with his chin resting on the footrest of the chair.

The phone rang. He decided to let his answering service get it. They didn't. Hardy cursed the goof-offs for not doing their job and picked up the phone. He started to say hello but he remembered he was a detective looking for work again.

"Trouble Limited, Patrick Hardy speaking."

108

"Mr. Hardy, this is James Norse."

"Mr. Norse, have you seen today's papers?"

"Yes, I have. I was wondering if you had."

"Yes sir," said Hardy, "which means I won't be getting in your hair from now on. My only interest was that Kate's killer be found. Now that they've got that kid, I'll never go near that block again."

"I'm very glad to hear that."

"Is there anything else I can do for you?"

"Yes. Be a man of your word. Goodbye."

As Hardy hung up his stomach began to ache, and it wasn't from the martinis. "That's all I need on top of everything else. Stomach spasms."

He was about to leave his desk and go to either the barber chair or the chaise when the phone rang again.

"Trouble Limited. Patrick Hardy speaking."

"Oh, that's adorable. You mean thing. I thought you were going to call me."

"Oh, hi Sue."

" 'Oh, hi Sue.' Is that the best you can do? Yesterday I was a great movie star you couldn't do enough for, today I'm just another broad you laid."

"That's not it, and you know it. I've got this terrible hangover."

"Well, why don't you come over here and let me take care of it . . . I promise I won't make you drink any more of my martinis. It's all my fault. Sometimes they can be lethal. Are you coming over?"

"When?"

"Right now, of course, and this time I'll let you smear my makeup.

Despite his hung-over condition and queasy stomach, he had an immediate erection. "As soon as I can."

He was about to strip to get into the tub when the phone rang again.

"Hello."

"Hi, Pat."

"Hello, Denny."

"I'm sorry I didn't call sooner, but I've been busy."

Hardy looked at the desk clock. As usual, it had stopped. He decided to skip the bath. "That's all right, Den."

"Oh, Pat, you're not supposed to say that."

"What am I supposed to say?"

"You're supposed to say that you've been worried sick and why the hell didn't I get back to you sooner."

He massaged his neck. "Right. Consider it said."

"You bastard. Pat . . . I'm not doing anything tonight. Do you want to come here or should I come up to your place?"

"Gee kid, I'm sorry, but I've got something on for tonight."

"That's okay. Just thought I'd ask. Another time, okay?"

"Okay," and they both hung up the phone. Pat sat down again. His stomachache was worse. He really liked that girl. He thought about calling her back, but then he thought about those marvelous breasts waiting for him, and the first thought was gone as quickly as it had come.

He ran the electric razor over his face and soaped his armpits clean in the sink. He followed this with a liberal application of Brut and put on a clean T-shirt. After much deliberation, he left his walking stick at home.

The cab ride was smooth and comfortable, considering the state his head was in. What bothered him was that the vagrant thought of taking a look around Madison Street kept flitting through his head.

Hardy made a face at himself and lit a cigarette. It tasted awful. He flicked it out the window.

He overtipped the cabdriver and strode into the hotel lobby. Before going to the desk, he stopped at the newstand and bought a pack of chewing gum. He took out a piece and chewed it vigorously for several minutes. His mouth didn't taste much better, but he hoped it smelled better. He threw the wad of gum into a sand-filled urn and went to the desk to get Sue's room number.

"I'm sorry, we are not allowed to divulge that information," said the prissy type.

Hardy couldn't believe his eyes or his ears. The man looked like Franklin Pangborn, the actor who had played all those desk clerks in the '40s' movies. He talked like a 1940s' movie, too. Hardy welcomed himself to the Twilight Zone and tried again. "Would you call her, please, and tell her that Patrick Hardy is here."

The man twisted his face in what seemed to be amiable disdain and did as Hardy asked.

The face twisted again, and now the clerk was all smiles. "You may go up, sir. Sorry, but we do get such crazy people coming in, and . . . well, you know how it is."

"No, how is it?" said Hardy, doing his best Groucho Marx imitation. "What's the room number?"

The sneer was sneaking back, but the man told him, and Hardy went for the nearest elevator, automatically lighting another cigarette.

He stubbed it out when he reached Sue's floor. At her door he glanced around to see if the hall was empty. Satisfied, he tucked in his shirt and rearranged the knot in his tie and smoothed his hair. It was only after he had rung her bell and was standing there waiting that he remembered that he still had that damned weight hanging around his left ankle.

The door opened.

She was wearing a peignoir. He didn't know what she had on underneath it but he hoped.

"Champagne," she said and pointed to the bottle resting in the ice-filled bucket. He winced at the thought of more alcohol in his system but he nodded.

"You do the honors," she said, "while I set the mood."

She drew the blinds and turned on several lamps that had red bulbs in them. Hardy wondered at this woman and fumbled with the tinfoil and twisted wire. His head was able to sustain the pop of the cork but drum music on the phonograph was a bit of a shock.

He poured the champagne and they each drank a glass and he repoured, feeling slightly better.

She tasted her second glass, smiled, put it down and stood up . . . and dropped her robe to the floor.

She was wearing the cave woman outfit she had worn in the movie, or at least one just like it. Hardy gaped in amazement. She jumped up onto a table and struck a pose that had been used for the poster of the movie, the one that had made her famous.

Hardy didn't know what else to do so he applauded.

Sue glared angrily and grunted something.

Nonplussed, he blurted, "Great, just like the movie."

Sue grunted again and made cave woman gestures.

He got the message. It was playacting time. He gulped his champagne down and stripped off his clothes. He was down to his shorts and his two-pound weight and trying to figure what to do about the latter when she jumped him.

As they rolled around the floor and she tore off his shorts, Hardy forgot about it and concentrated on the problem of the moment.

His shorts were gone and so was the top half of her outfit. The red light permeated the room and the drums were beating and the cave girl was grunting . . . and so was Hardy as they thrashed around and his eyes and his body and his hands and his mouth made contact with America's gift to mankind, Susannah Dow's monumental breasts.

More clothing tore and further contact was made, and made, and made and made.

He awoke to find her licking the sweat from his chest. And they fought another round.

And what seemed like minutes later, a third.

At her fourth attack he murmured, "Umgowa . . . which means I quit. Sorry, baby, that's it for me."

She persisted, but when she saw that nothing would come of it, she leaned back against the coffee table and lit a cigarette and said, "That's why it's always better with two men. They can spell each other. Don't fret about it, my dear. It's really my problem, not yours. I mean, don't go around feeling inadequate . . . you are certainly more than adequate. It's just that I need . . . well, you know what I need. I remember one night when Gary and Ralph . . . never mind. That's in the past, and you have to live for today. Right?"

"Right," and he turned to catch forty winks on the floor.

"I'm sorry, darling, but I'm going to have to ask you to leave now. I don't want to give the hotel people more to gossip about than is necessary."

She kissed him gently on the lips and surprised Hardy by saying, "Gosh." He didn't expect that expression from anyone nowadays, least of all Susannah Dow.

"Gosh," she repeated, "I sure hope I pegged you right and you're not a showoff with a big mouth."

He kissed her back. "Umgowa . . . which means, don't worry, your secret is safe with me."

"Good, I'm glad. I don't really give a damn what they say about me, it would probably help my box office, but as long as Peter is working for the government, I have to be what is known as circumspect. I'm leaving for the Coast tomorrow. I could give you a ring when I get back, that is if you wouldn't mind bringing a friend along next time. If you have a twin brother, he would be perfect."

Hardy didn't say a word. He took the cigarette from her mouth and smoked it and placed it back in her mouth. He didn't dig the idea of a threesome with another man involved, another woman wouldn't be so bad, but another man . . . still he didn't want to cut off his supply of Susannah Dow. He kept silent and picked up his things and went to the bathroom to shower and dress. He laughed when he noticed the leg weight.

After showering and dousing himself with Sue's bath powder, he strapped the weight back, put on his clothing and came back to find her wrapped in her peignoir again.

At the door he said, "Don't worry, Sue, I won't tell a soul, but you have to tell me something."

"What's that?"

"You talked about a night with Gary and `Ralph . . ."

She frowned.

"Relax," he went on, "just one question. Was that night you mentioned this past Christmas Eve?"

He stood in the doorway waiting for an answer.

She stood there biting the inside of her cheek. Finally she shrugged. "What the hell," she whispered. "Yes."

114

Chapter Twelve

Terry Hyde was waiting for him when he stepped out into the street to flag a cab.

"Hello, Mr. Hardy. Need a lift? Glad to oblige. The Boss's car is right over here."

Hardy's eyes darted in every direction trying to decide which way to run when Hyde let him see the gun he was concealing in his coat pocket.

Another man was waiting in the driver's seat.

"In the back," said Hyde.

When they were situated, one of his ringed hands picked up the phone. "You know where, Fletch. Let's go."

Hyde took a flask from his pocket. "Have a drink?"

"No thanks."

"Drink it."

Hardy did as he was told.

"More," commanded Hyde.

Again he obeyed.

His legs were very heavy. The weight. He should take the weight off, it was too heavy. He didn't know what to do. His arms were heavy. He had to do something. The cave men were coming. The cave men were coming. His head was very heavy. He . . .

When he awoke his wrists were tied behind him. He was groggy. There was a window. He peered through it. It was still night. His head was starting to clear, and he realized he was in the back of a parked panel truck. He pushed against the rear door. Locked. Of course.

It was cold.

He sat down and tried to think. The thoughts would not come. They hadn't tied his legs. He pushed his hands down as far as they could go and got his good leg through. He tried to get the bad leg through the same way, but it just wouldn't bend enough. And it hurt. At least the pain he had caused the leg took his mind off the cold. But now he was in a worse position than before, semi-bent over with his hands tied around his bad leg.

He couldn't tell what it was, but there was some sort of metal protrusion on the wall of the truck. It wasn't sharp, but it was all he had, and it was low enough for him to reach.

After an hour of rubbing away at the rope, he had frayed it a lot, but was nowhere near getting loose and his back ached from the constant bending over. His head was clearer now but not much.

He sat down to rest and started worrying about the time. They might never come back or could be back any moment.

And he had a desperate urge to take a leak.

Suppressing the urge as best he could, he concentrated on getting out of the truck.

If he had his hands in front of him, he might have a

116

chance of forcing that lock. He tried again. No way. The pain was unbearable.

He stopped and caught his breath. One more thought. He turned his back to the double doors and using his rear end as a battering ram, he started butting away. All the time thinking how stupid he was to be concerned with the pun of his use of his butt to butt the door.

It worked. After nearly tumbling into the gutter, he hobbled down and started making his way along the street.

"Going some place, Mr. Hardy?"

It was Terry Hyde. Next to him was Fletch, the man who had driven the limousine. Fletch circled around. Now Hyde was behind him and Fletch was in front of him and he was in the middle tied up like a calf in a Western movie. He knew Hyde had the gun. Fletch? An undetermined factor. But by now Hardy's thinking process was becoming less cerebral and more reflexive.

He catapulted himslf toward Fletch and butted him in the stomach. He didn't think of the pun this time. His mind was too busy hiding from all this violence. Fletch was down. Hardy started to turn but by this time Hyde had tapped him behind the ear with the barrel of his gun.

Out he went again.

This time when he awoke he was in a room sitting on a couch. Hyde was there, as well as James Victor Norse. Fletch was nowhere to be seen. Hardy hoped he was dead, but he imagined he was outside the door keeping guard.

Hyde had replaced the gun with a knife and when Hardy awoke he gestured toward the detective.

"Just give me the word, Mr. Norse."

117

"Back off, Terry."

They both appeared to be drunk or high or something, Hardy didn't know what. He was still groggy from the last two days' experience with Sue and whatever Hyde had had in his flask and the bop on the head he had received. No man of action now, merely a very frightened man. He was still as he had been on the street with both hands tied around his left thigh.

Norse was talking. "I want to tell you something, Mr. Wise Guy. You messed up a very nice little enterprise I had going for me. For that alone I ought to let Terry finish you. But that's not why you're here. I've known you long enough not to like you. I'm a pretty good judge of character. I know something else about you. In a couple of days you would start figuring that maybe that Spic kid didn't kill Kate and then you would be nosing into my business again. I don't need that. For your information, I was taking care of her. She was a nice girl. I liked her. I gave her money and got her a lot of nice clothes. You should have seen the last dress I got her, a pretty blue one with white trim on the collar. She looked nice in that . , . I gave it to her the day before she died. . . . I didn't kill her either. I loved her. In a different way than anyone could know.

"Not the way you Broadway studs mean it. I loved her . . . and I didn't kill her."

The man's rambling barely made sense. Hardy tried to get comfortable.

"Don't move," said Hyde.

"You still have a chance," said Norse. "If you can get me to believe you're so scared of what might happen to you that you will lay off . . . completely, I might let you walk out of here."

118

Hyde didn't seem to like that. "Mr. Norse, what are you talking about?"

"Too many corpses make the cops too nosy. If we come to an understanding, he lives."

"Fine," said Hardy quickly. "Anything you say."

Hyde wasn't happy at all. "Don't believe him, Mr. Norse. He's got to die."

"Nonsense."

"He knows we killed that Bishop guy because he was blackmailing you about what was going on in this building."

"Don't try to provoke me, Terry. I'm angry enough as it is. Now at you as well as Mr. Hardy. Word from the top is to keep killings to a minimum. He doesn't know a thing. He only knows what you said, and he will keep his mouth shut about that as well as everything else, and he will stop all poking around . . . and he will forget I ever existed and for that favor, he can live."

A sadistic gleam came into Terry Hyde's eyes, and he pointed with the knife. "What if he knew that when you said you loved that girl in a different way than anyone could know, you meant because you couldn't do it the way normal men do it? What if he knew you were impotent?"

Norse screamed in rage. "Goddamn it, Terry. Now you have to kill him." He crossed over to his hireling and slapped him in the face and screamed again, "Kill him."

Hardy's adrenaline was back in action. Using the same tactic he had used in the street, he dove head first at Norse's back. Norse's scream of rage became one of pain and death as he was skewered by Hyde's knife.

Hardy tucked himslef into a ball and tolled away

and then added his own scream of pain as he forced his bad leg through his bound hands.

Norse was on the floor, the knife in his chest.

Hyde was standing next to his body.

Hardy was opposite, his bound hands now in front.

Hyde had time to retrieve his knife, but he chose not to and advanced on Hardy.

Hyde kept his hands moving in all directions as he came. Had Hardy's imagination been functioning, the flashing rings would have seemed menacing. But his imagination and his thinking process were hiding in a little corner of his brain. At the forefront were the instincts and the reflexes the Army had sharpened for him years before.

Hyde feinted with a left hand. Hardy didn't move. Hyde stepped in fast, thrusting out a vicious right hand. Hardy grabbed at it and pulled it around Hyde's back. He had the armlock, now he pulled and twisted, trying to break the right arm or damage the shoulder socket before Hyde could do any damage with his left or with his feet.

Hardy wasn't fast enough. Hyde did just that. With his free left hand, he aimed a blow at Hardy's groin. The blow was off its mark and hammered on Hardy's left knee.

Hardy screamed in pain again and relaxed enough for Hyde to toss Hardy over his back and across the room and into the wall.

Hardy lay there in a heap. Through half-open eyes he saw Hyde coming in for the kill. He had to get up. He couldn't.

Then he felt something under his bound hands. They were resting on his left ankle. They were resting on the two-pound weight that was wrapped around his left ankle.

Hyde was starting to lean over to hoist Hardy to his feet. Hardy pulled at the velcro fastening. He ripped the two pounds from his leg. Its own momentum arced the weight back over Hardy's head. He swung it forward and smashed it right into Hyde's descending face. This time it was Hyde who screamed and passed out.

Hardy readied himself as the door opened and the man Fletch poked his head in. The man surveyed the scene and ran. Hardy fainted. Only seconds later he awoke. When he saw the mess he wanted to run, too. He turned his eyes away from Hyde's battered face and tried not to retch. He looked at the bloody two-pound weight in his hand and let it fall to the floor.

Slowly he rose to his feet and forced himself to go to Norse's body to remove the knife and use it to cut the ropes around his wrists.

He searched out the toilet where he urinated. He drank a lot of water and urinated again. Then he washed his face and went about the apartment until he found a telephone.

After calling the police, he made himself check the room where the two bodies were. He didn't want to but he knew he had to check and see whether or not Hyde was shamming.

He wasn't. He was unconscious, but alive. Norse was dead.

Satisfied but not happy, Hardy left the room and closed the door behind him and waited for the police to arrive.

Chapter Thirteen

After the police had carted James Victor Norse off to the morgue and Terry Hyde to the hospital and sent out a description on Fletch and Hardy had answered all their questions and had been looked at by the police doctor, he left the building and walked.

He wasn't going anywhere, he merely wanted to walk. He was tired but he seemed to feel the need for movement rather than sleep. While he walked he tried to sort things out. They wouldn't sort. He would leave that for another day. One thought did occur as he saw the first glimmers of the morning sun trying to break through New York's atmosphere. It was Thursday. If he went home to sleep, Laura would be there soon with her vacuum cleaner and her conversations with her television shows. He'd never get any rest.

He had walked to midtown. He checked into the Americana Hotel, called his service to have them call Laura and explain that everything was all right and that she should leave food out for Holmes before she left in case he wasn't back by that time.

He made doubly sure that the "Do Not Disturb" sign was on his door, and he told the hotel operator not to let any calls through. Chores done, he shed his clothes and crawled under the covers of the hotel bed. His last thoughts before he fell into an exhausted sleep were how very hungry he was.

Thursday night when he got home, he locked all the locks and made himself a huge salami sandwich. With that and a large bottle of cream soda, he ensconced Holmes and himself on the chaise and turned on the TV and turned off the world.

The phone rang several times, but he paid no attention and let the service handle it.

He slept late on Friday, rejecting all thoughts of working out or even of going out. Ignoring the stack of mail Laura had placed on his desk, he made two calls. One for an appointment with Dr. Merle Doyle, the other for an appointment with Dr. Ward Nesor. They were both for Monday.

When the phone rang this time, he picked it up without thinking.

"Good morning, Mr. Hardy. Do you recognize my voice?"

He remembered. The tape machine in his head gave him instant replay. It had been the day Ben Pelligrin had killed Peg and Hardy had killed Pelligrin.

He had taken the suitcase full of money and was walking along the street when Mrs. White's chauffeured black car cruised along beside him.

His mind tape kept playing. "Get in, Mr. Hardy."

He'd gotten in next to Mr. White.

"I believe, Mr. Hardy, that you have my property." Mr. White had relieved him of the suitcase. "We have been aware of Mr. Pelligrin's duplicity for a long time. You have been a great source of annoyance to me, Mr. Hardy, but you have also done me a great service."

The mental memory tape took only a second to run its course. Hardy spoke into the phone to answer one of "The Organization's" highest ranking men. "Yes, Mr. Whi . . ."

"Please, Mr. Hardy, your careless tongue. It's still wagging too much. Mr. W. will suffice."

"Yes, Mr. W."

"It seems that once more you have involved yourself in my affairs. You know how much I dislike that. But it also seems that once more you have done me a service and come away unscathed. Thanks to your efforts there is a man now lying dead in the morgue. This man had been stepping on my toes, so to speak. For this I thank you. While you were out an envelope was left with your housekeeper. If it bothers your conscience, give it away or burn it, I don't care. Know this, too. I did not like the man who now lies in the morgue, therefore my gratitude, but had he been an associate in good standing, my reaction would have been completely the reverse. You were lucky again, Mr. Hardy. But from now on may I suggest you confine your work to areas that do not infringe on my domain. Do I make myself clear?"

"Yes, Mr. W."

"Goodbye."

Hardy picked up the batch of envelopes from his desk. The yellow one on top had a note from Laura clipped to it explaining that it had been hand-delivered. Hardy opened it and counted out the five thousand dollars.

The thought of blood money did enter his mind, but only briefly. He left his desk to go to the wall safe behind the George Grosz drawing. He opened the safe and tossed the money inside. Then he closed it and absent-mindedly woolgathered as he twirled the knob repeatedly. The wool he gathered was ugly. James Norse and Terry Hyde had been bad enough, but Mr. W. filled him with sheer terror.

125

He wrenched his mind from his thoughts and his hand from the knob and covered the safe again with the drawing. Now he stood back and admired the craft of the German artist. What sort of picture would George Grosz draw of him, he wondered.

He went to the kitchen to get some food.

When he had finished eating, he went to the closet and fixed the phone bell so he wouldn't hear it at all.

He hibernated fot the rest of the weekend. This time not even bothering to go out for the Sunday papers.

Monday he fixed the phone bell, called his service, received the messagés, including several from Denise Shaw and one from Gerald Friday, and took Holmes for a long morning romp.

All this taken care of, he walked the several blocks downtown to Merle Doyle's office.

The sight of his pretty doctor always made him feel better. Hardy had been trying to make her for years but with no success. He admired the way her brown hair rippled as she shook her head.

"Pat, I don't know what I'm going to do with you."

"I have a suggestion."

"Oh, keep quiet. Your pressure is back up again."

"Well, I have been under a bit of a strain," and he continued telling her the story he had started when he had first come in. When he was through, she turned up her radio to enjoy a section of Mahler. They both listened to the music for a moment and then she said, "I think you should change your line of work."

"You and Mr. W."

"Who?"

"Never mind. What about the rest of me?"

"A few bruises here and there, nothing serious. Knee looks okay to me, but you should have Nesor look at it. Have you just gotten over a cold?"

"No."

"Well, then you're going to get one in the next few days."

"How can you tell that?"

She smiled and turned down the radio. "We have our ways. I'll give you a prescription for more tranquilizers. Take them. Keep that pressure down. While I'm at it, I'll also give you a prescription for that head cold you'll probably get."

"Gee thanks, Doc."

"Don't mention it," and she smiled again. "If I'm wrong, just tear it up . . . knowing you, you'll get them just to take anyway. If you use them, they might make you a little sleepy so don't drive or anything like that."

He looked at his watch. "Thanks for everything. I've got to run across town and get to Doctor Nesor's."

"Wait a minute. I knew I forgot something. I forgot to weigh you."

"Sorry, I'm in a big rush."

"You should be no more than one hundred eighty pounds and right now you look about ten pounds overweight . . . well?"

Having no answer, he groped for a cigarette.

"And cut down on the smoking."

"I want to tell you that this has been a wonderful experience being here today with you."

"Me, too. Bye." And she turned up the radio again.

His visit to Dr. Nesor was shorter.

"No problem here, Pat. As a matter of fact, I'm very pleased with the way the knee is coming along. Good-looking scar if I do say so myself."

"How long before everything's back to normal?"

"Let's get one thing straight. That knee will never be normal. You can build up the muscle by exercise

127

and cut down the chances of it ever going out again, but cartilage does not grow back."

"Gee thanks, Doc," said Hardy, mocking his own earlier remark to Merle Doyle.

"But with the right therapy we can be ninety percent sure."

Hardy relaxed. "That's good enough for me. What do I do?

Nesor wiped his glasses. "Keep bending it in the tub and keep doing those knee shrug exercises to strengthen the quadricep muscles. I like the leg weight, it's a good idea."

Hardy grimaced. He hadn't mentioned to Nesor the special use he had made of it.

Nesor was still talking. "I want you to go see a therapist. She's a trifle nuts but she knows what she's doing."

He kept talking as he wrote. "Her name is Natasha Tamarova, used to be a ballerina. She's got a studio at the Grand Central Terminal building. Getting there the first time is complicated. I'll write it out for you. It's more like a combination gym and dance studio. You'll love it. Tell her hello for me. Give yourself about two months before you go to her. Now get out of here. I don't want to see you around here any more." And he handed Hardy the slip of paper and went on to his next patient.

Hardy got dressed, paid his bill and left. As he walked along, much to his own disgust, he was glad for the five thousand dollars Mr. W. had sent. His bank balance had gotten much too low.

At home he was just in time to watch an old Mickey Rooney movie, *The Strip*. Louis Armstrong and Jack Teagarden and "Fatha" Hines were in it and Hardy dug their music. Besides "Basin Street" and a couple of other jazz things, they played a ballad that Hardy had always liked, "A Kiss to Build a Dream On." It was a good song, and Hardy being the kind of sentimentalist such songs were written for, got turned on by it.

He went to the phone and called Denise.

"Long time no hear from," she said.

"Yeah, well, I've been kind of busy."

"Care to tell me about it?"

"I'd love to."

"Good," she said, "I'd love to hear it."

"That's nice," he said. "Would you like to come up here?"

"A gentleman would offer to come down here."

"I'm sorry, Den, I wasn't thinking. I'll. . ."

"Don't be a jerk," she answered. "I'll be there in twenty minutes."

Whenever Hardy knew a movie was going to have music he liked, he taped it. He had done this with the music from the Rooney movie and had it set up on the machine for when Denise showed up. He knew it wasn't necessary, but he kind of liked the idea of doing it.

He pulled a couple of steaks from the freezer and poured himself a scotch and skimmed through Jules Feiffer's *Great Comic Book Heroes* to kill time until Denise arrived.

He was surprised that Holmes didn't bark when the phone rang. Hardy looked down and there was the poodle waiting patiently for him to answer it. As he went to his desk to do so, Hardy reasoned that the dog's calmness was reflecting his own. Feeling very good about that, he answered the phone.

"Hello," he started and then corrected it to announce his business name, "Trouble . . ."

Friday didn't let him finish. "Hello trouble?" The cop laughed. "If I'd been through what you've been through, I guess I'd be answering my phone the same way." He laughed again. "Hello trouble, if you're not doing anything tomorrow why don't you drop by and fill me in on a few things. I've got to take the precinct report and Homicide's report and collate it into a special comprehensive report for the people at the top. There are a few blank spots."

"Sure thing. Hey . . . what I said about that Puerto Rican kid . . ."

"Forget it. You might not have been too far off the mark at that. I zinged you, you zinged me. We're even."

"Okay, Gerry, see you tomorrow about two o'clock."

"Wait a minute, Private Detective. When did we get on a first-name basis?"

"Just now, I guess."

"Well, if we're such great pals, you'd better make it one o'clock and we can have lunch. There's a great Chinese restaurant up here and since you're such a good pal, Pat my friend, I'm going to let you treat."

"Right. Tomorrow at one."

The doorbell rang just as he hung up. This time Holmes did bark. Hardy went to let Denise in . . . then he stopped himself and ran back to turn the tape on.

"Give me a kiss to build a dream on, and my imagination. . ."

Now he went to the door and let her in. With the song as entrance background music, he held her hand and led her in. The trouble was that Holmes was dancing around her and taking all of her attention and destroying the mood.

While she kissed and fondled the dog and made greeting noises to it and got out of her coat, Hardy ran the tape back and tried again.

She hugged him and they kissed softly and sweetly.

130

"It's nice to see you again," she murmured into his ear.

"I like what I see, too."

"Okay," and her face beamed.

"Okay. You want a drink?"

"Red wine, if you have any."

"How could I forget. Specialty of the house."

He turned off the tape and switched to an F.M. music station and gave her the wine.

"You hungry?" He sat next to her on the couch.

"Not yet. You?"

"No," he answered and kissed her again.

She kissed him back but said, "Pat, could we just sit here and hold hands and cuddle and just talk."

"Sure thing. After all, what's the rush? We've got all night."

While they sat and cuddled and drank and talked, he told her most of the events that had led to the showdown with Norse and Hyde. She made the proper remarks and exclamations and kissed him even more tenderly. "To take away the hurt," she explained.

Then she interrupted herself. "Poor David . . . well now that it's all over, what are you going to do?"

"Get another job as soon as I can. No, that's a lie. Not as soon as I can. Like you said before, what's the rush?"

"Pat . . . about Gary."

"Forget it, it's a closed book."

"Are you sure?"

"Absatively and posolutely."

She giggled. "Silly," and they went back to their kissing and cuddling.

Soon the kissing and cuddling became more ardent and they didn't get to their steak dinner until much much later on.

In the morning she insisted on making breakfast for

131

him. The eggs were fried a little too hard and the bacon wasn't crisp enough, but he never said a word. They parted with sweet kisses and promises to call each other.

He sat in the barber chair and smoked quietly and contentedly while he sipped a second cup of coffee. After waiting fifteen minutes, he went to the gym for a strenuous workout, really enjoying the increasing strength of his left leg. He took another shower and then napped until it was time for him to get dressed.

He took the bus up to the Ninety-seventh Street stop and walked the rest of the way. He felt pretty good and smiled at the fact of it.

He smiled again when the Chinese restaurant Gerald Friday took him to turned out to be one on One hundred twenty-seventh Street and one Hardy had been going to ever since his college days.

"Hello, Mr. Friday. Two for lunch?"

"Right, Henry," said the stocky black cop.

"What's the matter, Henry," Hardy asked, "no hello for me?"

The Chinese waiter peered myopically at him. "Mr. Hardy. Good to see you. Long time no see."

Henry fussed over him as he led them to their table.

After they had ordered their beef in black bean sauce and sweet and sour chicken and fried dumplings, Friday started off.

"First, let me fill you in. Hyde's in bad shape but he'll live. When he goes to trial, the D.A. will probably want you to testify."

"No problem."

"No trace of the other man, Fletch, but the same goes for him if and when we get him."

"Right."

The dumplings arrived first. Hardy picked up the soy sauce bottle and showed it to Friday.

132

"Yeah, sure, pour it on. Now talk."

Hardy took a bite of dumpling. "My mother told me never to talk with my mouth full."

Friday shook his head. "Wise-ass."

"Okay," said Hardy, "I'm not going to tell you about the fight. I don't even want to think about it." He shuddered and took another forkful.

"Come on, give," said Friday, "And leave some of those for me."

"Norse had some sort of racket going on in that building. What it was, I don't know. That's for you to find out. Bishop either saw something or figured it out. Anyway, he was putting the bite on Norse. Norse paid for a while, but Bishop must have gotten greedy so Norse had Hyde shoot him. Again, that's your problem."

The rest of their order arrived.

Friday watched Hardy working with the chopsticks, taking bits of food from each serving dish and passing it to the bowl of rice in front of him from which he shoveled the mixture into his mouth.

"Showoff," said the cop and then proceeded to eat in the same fashion but with a lot more skill.

"Big deal," said Hardy and kept eating.

Friday swallowed a mouthful and said, "Less eat, more talk."

Hardy poured them both some tea. He looked around to make sure that Henry wasn't watching and added some sugar to his cup. "He doesn't like it when I do that."

"Talk."

"Anyway . . ." He sipped his tea. "Hot . . . anyway, Norse was keeping the girl, but only keeping her. He never laid a hand on her, sexually or otherwise. He was impotent."

Hardy stopped while ugly memory pictures flashed

133

through his head. "Knowing that is what nearly got me killed. So that would eliminate him as a suspect in Kate's murder. Bishop is dead, but we know where he was so that eliminates him. This next part is strictly off the record. As they say in government, for your ears only. The reason Thorpe and Price gave such rotten alibis is that they were lying . . . to protect a friend. The two of them were forming a trio in the sack with a very kinky but a very nice lady. Trouble is she's married, and if it ever got out, it would be very bad news for the lady and her husband. Those two jokers were just being gallant."

"Who was the woman?"

"Never mind."

"Come on, Pat, who was the woman?"

"If you ever need to know officially, I'll tell you. Now lay off. I gave my word."

Friday looked annoyed and they ate silently for a few moments.

"Goddamn it, Pat. Who is she?"

"Forget it. So that eliminates Norse and Bishop and Price and Thorpe. You have Hyde and you have to prove that he killed Bishop, but that's your problem. Mine is who killed Kate."

They both looked up and stared at each other as he said the last.

"What the hell's the matter with you, Pat? Carlos Ortega did it. We have his confession."

"That's right," said Hardy, "the Spanish kid did it." But even as he said it he knew his subconscious remark was a signal to himself that he really didn't believe it at all.

Chapter Fourteen

Wednesday morning when he woke up he had a cold. Coughing and wheezing and blowing his nose, he forced himself to get dressed and get out. Holmes barked that he wanted to come, too, but Hardy was too miserable to think about anyone but himself.

He rushed into Hank Bianco's drugstore, then fidgeted while he waited for the gossipy old man in front of him to be through.

"Hi, Pat, how are you?"

"Hello, Hank, why do all doctors and druggists always ask that question with sadistic anticipation?"

"I give up, you tell me."

"Never mind, could you fill this prescription for me?"

"Sure, take about a half hour."

Hardy blew his nose. "Come on, have a heart. I don't even think I'll be alive in a half hour."

"All right," said Hank, "fifteen minutes."

"I know if I waited," coughed Hardy, "you could get it done in five, but if I stay here that long the

Board of Health would close you down. Be back in ten minutes." And he went outside and walked around trying to breathe.

When he came back in less than ten minutes, Hank handed him a little paper bag and said, "What took you so long?"

"Very funny. Very funny. Put it on my bill."

"Now that's funny. You haven't paid your bill in four months."

"Send it to my lawyer, my estate will take care of it . . . after my death which will take place in approximately one hour."

Hank looked sympathetic. "Take care, Pat. Yes, Ma'am, can I help you?"

Hardy struggled back to Riverside Drive, washed one of the blue pills down and gargled with salt water and crawled back into bed.

Denise called and wanted to take care of him, but he warned her away. "No, honey. You might catch it. I'll be all right in a couple of days."

Then he called Laura. "So I think maybe you'd better skip tomorrow. I have this terrible cold and you might get it from me."

"Don't be silly, Mr. Hardy. Of course I'll come. I never catch anything like that. That's because I take care of myself, not like some people I know who stay out all hours of the night."

He groaned.

Laura went on. "I'll be there bright and early to make you breakfast and I'll make you some soup for lunch. That'll really perk you up."

Hardy groaned again. "No, Laura, I really don't think . . ." But she had hung up.

Thursday was a nightmare. When Laura wasn't vacuuming, she was talking to the TV, when she wasn't talking to the TV, she was talking to him, when she wasn't talking, she was pushing soup down his throat.

The phone rang and Laura picked it up.

"I don't want to speak to anyone," said Hardy.

Laura explained this to the phone and then said to Hardy, "It's a young lady. Her name is Denise."

"I'll take it. Hi, Den."

Denise coughed into his ear and said, "Guess what?"

Hardy croaked out a laugh. "I'm sorry, baby, I guess I gave it to you already."

"That's all right," she said, "It's better than what some fellows give their girls . . . if you feel as bad as I do, I know you don't want to talk any more. Bye."

And he hung up the phone and bravely waited out the day until Laura finally left.

By Monday he was fine, but Denise's cold was still hanging on.

Having nothing better to do, he went to a porno movie. While he was there he enjoyed it very much and even got turned on. But once outside the turn-on was gone and instead of thinking about sex, he thought about Carlos Ortega and Kate Arnheim. Or was that thinking about sex? Another problem for Dr. Freud.

He tried to pretend to himself that he was being absent-minded as he went to the Independent subway instead of the IRT and took a downtown train instead of an uptown one.

He got off at Delancey Street. He hadn't been in that particular section of town for a long time and wanted to get the feel of it.

Past the wool stores and the bodegas and the places that sold Jewish religious items and the park and the church and then back to the park where he sat and watched the kids fooling around on the outdoor basketball court. Black and Puerto Rican kids for the most part.

The older people had a larger share of Jews or so he assumed by their beards and their faces.

Hardy was troubled. He knew there wasn't a chance of anyone in this ghetto neighborhood giving him straight answers. He was an outsider and no pretense on his part could hide that. Giving it up as a lost cause, he went home.

There he went directly to his cork wall and reread all the information he had. Except for the Bowers' San Francisco address he tore everything up and typed a new list:

1. The Pritchetts

He exed that out and started over:

1. The fags.
2. Kate's mother.
3. Kate's stepfather.
4. 2 and 3 together.
5. Person or persons unknown.
6. Carlos Ortega.
7. Crap. Crap. And double crap.

He pulled the list from the typewriter and was going to tear it up but changed his mind and pinned it to the wall. He stared at it for some time, and then put a question mark next to number three. Kate's stepfather. What did he know about him?

He thumbed through his address book and found the number he wanted and dialed it.

"Glory Travel Service."

"Joan?"

"Yes."

"This is Pat, Pat Hardy."

"Hi, Pat, how are you?"

"Fine. How fast can you get me to San Francisco?"

138

"When do you want to leave?"

"Five minutes ago."

"Economy or first class."

"Just get me there."

"Right. Hold on."

He tapped on his desk with a pencil while he waited. He would have to take Holmes to the kennel. The poodle hated it there, but there was no time to get Laura to come over to get him.

"Hello?"

"Yes, Joan."

"Is three thirty okay?"

Hardy looked at his watch. "Great."

"All right. Hold on again."

He checked his cardcase to see that the credit cards were there, and he would take some of Mr. W.'s cash. Using it for a good cause would take some of the onus from it, at least that's what he told himself.

"Pat. . . ?"

He grunted affirmation.

"Okay. Be on your way. You're booked on flight number seven, TWA, it goes at three thirty from Kennedy."

Hardy hung up and called the kennel and made the necessary arrangements. He grabbed the rest of what he needed and the dog and rushed out, stopping long enough to make sure all his locks and alarms were set.

Holmes gave him a dirty look when he saw what was happening to him. The angry bark followed Hardy out as he returned to the cab he had told to wait for him.

"Kennedy Airport."

"Right," said the driver and they were off.

Hardy made the terminal in plenty of time for a snack and then was sorry he had eaten it. He bought a pack of Tums at a stand and fed them to his complaining stomach and grabbed at several paperbacks without checking their titles. As he was paying he also bought several chocolate bars and extra Marlboros.

The plane ride was pleasant and uneventful. Hardy slept through most of it. When they landed, he checked into the closest accommodation and had food sent to his room. The private detective tried to formulate what he would say to the Bowers . . . how he would approach them.

As Hardy dried himself off, he planned to call them for an appointment, but his nap on the plane had made him more tired than less and the bath had been no help.

He lay down for a short rest.

Tuesday morning's California sunshine streamed through the window and right into his eyes. Hardy awoke. He felt good. Yawning and mumbling to himself about needing that sleep he showered and dressed.

It was nine o'clock. Hardy tried the Bowers' number. No answer. As he ate breakfast he had visions of going to this new address and finding them gone again. He dismissed all such notions and ordered a second cup of coffee.

After trying to reach them all day long, he connected. A woman answered.

"Mrs. Bower?"

"Yes?"

"You are the Mrs. Bower who was Kate Arnheim's mother?"

Hardy thought he heard a catch in her voice. "Yes."

"My name is Patrick Hardy. I'm in San Francisco and I was . . ."

"Oh, yes, Katrina mentioned you. I thought you live in New York, Mr. Hardy . . ."

At this point he heard another voice, a man's voice, further away from the phone. She had obviously covered the mouthpiece but it sounded like an argument. Whatever it was, it was short-lived.

"Yes, Mr. Hardy."

"First I'd like to say how sorry I am that I couldn't come to the funeral, I . . .

"That's all right. The flowers were very beautiful, I know Katrina would understand that you were her friend in death as well as in life."

"That's why I'm calling, Mrs. Bower. I'm sorry if I'm not saying this right, I know how painful it must be for you to talk about it, but would it be all right if I came over to see you."

"Why, Mr. Hardy?"

"I'm trying to find out who killed your daughter."

"They have the man, Mr. Hardy. They caught him after he killed another poor girl."

He could hear the emotion building in the woman.

"I'm sorry, Mrs. Bower, I don't think they have the right man."

Chapter Fifteen

There had been another argument on the other side of the phone while Hardy hung on. Finally the woman consented to his visit.

He pulled the rented car up the driveway and got out. He took several last puffs of his cigarette before he extinguished it. Then he took a deep breath and rang the bell of the neat white house.

Mrs. Bower looked so much like Kate it truly upset Hardy. She looked as though she had been crying, which upset him even more.

"Mr. Hardy, this is my husband, Mr. Bower."

"How do you do?"

Bower tossed off a hello and sat in an armchair. Hardy was surprised by his appearance. For some reason he had expected to see a burly giant of a man with hamlike hands and a close-cropped haircut. The man was long and lean and despite the way he talked and acted, his appearance was aristocratic. So much for cliché concepts.

"Mrs. Bower, and you too, Mr. Bower, I was wondering if there was anything you might tell me that would help in my investigation."

"I'm sorry, Mr. Hardy, I'm still not too clear on what you meant about them having the wrong man."

"I don't know about the other girl, but I don't think Carlos Ortega killed your daughter."

"You mean raped and killed," said Mr. Bower, shaking his head. "The nerve of you trying to get that spic off. He killed her, they should kill him. They should kill the whole lot of them. On second thought, maybe he didn't rape her. She probably let him. She let anyone. Do you know that she put out for niggers? If there was ever a girl who deserved God's vengeance, it was that girl."

"Please, Carl, don't."

"Don't Carl me. You know as well as I . . ."

Partly out of embarrassment and partly because he was thinking, Hardy tuned out on the argument. His cliché thinking might not have been that far wrong after all. Maybe Carl Bower did kill his stepdaughter.

Bower was talking to him. "Why don't you get out and leave us alone. We left New Jersey to get away from the shame, and you drag it all the way here to our door again."

"One question. May I ask where the two of you were Christmas Eve?"

Bower spit his answer, "At church and then at home, with the family, the way everyone should spend Christmas Eve. She was supposed to be with us, but then she said, no, she wasn't coming. Well, God punished her. She got what she deserved. Now, get out."

Mrs. Bower looked pained and said nothing.

Hardy halfheartedly gestured with his hand and tried to think of something to say to the woman.

"Get out I said. Leave my house," the man ordered.

Outside he mentally scratched Carl Bower's name from his list. He might have been happy about Kate's death, but he didn't do it. As he put the car into gear, Hardy pondered on Bower's comments on the way to spend Christmas Eve.

Being a lapsed Catholic troubled Hardy a great deal. His sometime agnostic mind wondered if Bower wasn't right. Was it God's punishment? Hardy pulled off to the side of the road. What the hell was he thinking about? Bower was a sick moralist who said all the righteous words and carried more evil around with him than five other people.

Hardy checked the traffic and got back onto the road and pulled into the first bar he could find.

Three scotches later and just as sober as when he had come in, he left and went back to his room and tried to sleep.

He dreamed about a Christmas party. Everybody was there. Hardy's father, and his mother, and his third grade teacher, and Angie Palmeri, the girl he had a crush on in junior high school, and Mr. W., and Norse and Hyde and Price and Thorpe, and Denise and Steve Macker and Ruby and Fried and McLean and Friday and Laura and Holmes and the Bowers and the Pritchetts. Everybody was having a good time around the tree. Everybody but Hardy. He pushed his way to get to the tree. Bit by bit, everyone left. Everyone, but one.

The Christmas tree wasn't a tree any more. It was Kate, the way she had looked that night, all bloody and dead. Hardy looked at Kate and then at the other person.

"You." His mouth formed the words, but there was no sound.

The other person nodded and vanished.

Hardy woke in a sweat and called the desk to prepare his bill. Then he made arrangements to get the first flight back to New York.

It was Wednesday night, New York time, when the plane got into landing position over Kennedy. After being stacked up for almost an hour, there was talk about going on to Boston, but the plane finally landed in New York.

It was too late to get Holmes out so Hardy went directly home. He slept fitfully having variations of his Christmas party dream.

In the morning he picked up the poodle and spent the day alone with him walking around getting food from frankfurter and taco and pizza vendors. Other than Holmes, Hardy was in no mood for any company, especially Laura's.

When he was sure the housekeeper would be gone, he went to the apartment. He would do what had to be done tomorrow.

He dreamed the same dream.

On Friday he got out of bed only long enough to look up "private investigators" in the Yellow Pages and called the first one he found with a Spanish name. He told Jose Hernandez what he needed. Then he went back and read himself to sleep.

Hernandez was fast. By two thirty he called back with his report.

Hardy yawned and rubbed his eyes. "Okay, shoot."

"You were right about Ortega and that girl. They went through the first three grades together. As dumb as it seems, from what I could pick up, he's had a crush on her all these years and never even went near her or told her about it. Then he flipped out and went to see her and raped her, and when she struggled, he cut her and killed her."

146

"And nobody ever told the police?" Hardy said almost gleefully.

"The cops never asked them. Some of them didn't even really remember it till I suggested it like you said."

"Which means Carlos Ortega had his own very real reason to rape that girl downtown. What was her name?"

"Rosa Torres."

"And that means he probably didn't kill Kate, and for some motive, lied about it," Hardy mumbled. Aloud, he said, "Look, Hernandez, you did a great job. Could you send me a written report on what you just said, with your bill?"

"Sure thing. Simple job. Just a little shoe leather. You were right to call me. They never would have told you any of it, even if you could talk Spanish. Can you?"

"No. And you're right. Look, I don't want to come on like a hot shot and embarrass you, but I think you deserve a bonus. Make the bill for two hundred instead of one."

"You don't embarrass me. Glad to take your money. Will you tell the cops or should I?"

"I will," said Hardy, "Adios."

"Yeah," said Hernandez, "so long."

Hardy checked his watch and told himself it could wait another day. It had waited this long. What was one more day?

That night he didn't dream at all.

On Saturday morning he called Denise and Ted McLean and Ronald Fried and Ralph Price and Gary Thorpe and Gerald Friday and Henry and Roberta Pritchett and invited them to come to his place that night for a party.

McLean at first refused, but fifteen minutes after Fried accepted, McLean called back to say he had changed his mind. The Pritchetts, too, were a little hesitant, but they finally said, yes, they would come.

They all said they would come.

Chapter Sixteen

When he was sure the party was on, Hardy called Friday a second time.

"Friend, I need a favor."

"You're getting it, I'm coming to your party."

"Careful, Gerry, you're starting to sound like me."

"God forbid. What's the favor?"

Hardy told him what Hernandez had reported and what the favor was and why.

"For Christ's sake, Pat, you did this to me once before. Number one, why didn't you tell me about Ortega yesterday? Two, it's my day off, and three, you know how tough it is to get a search warrant on a Saturday."

"Do it for the sake of black and white unity in America."

"I think I'll throw up," said the cop. "Somewhere there's got to be a protective society against private detectives."

"Will you do it?"

"Of course I'll do it. If you're right, I want this

damned mess cleared up as much as you do. More, as a matter of fact. I'm the one who's got to follow it up and untangle it all while you sit home and imitate some paperback hero." And he was off the line.

Hardy patted the phone affectionately and started his preparations for that night's festivities. It amused him when he realized he was actually whistling while he worked.

Denise showed first. Hardy allowed her to help him with whatever preparations were left to be made. Price arrived in a let-bygones-be-bygones mood, and Hardy fixed him a drink while Denise answered the door and showed the Pritchetts in.

Hardy banished Holmes to the bedroom. He knew how excited the animal got when people started yelling and making violent moves, and he was pretty sure that things would turn out that way.

He came back in time to pour drinks for the Pritchetts while Denise answered the door again. He had to suppress a smile when Henry and Roberta Pritchett lived up to his bartending expectations. Henry had the sherry on the rocks and Roberta had the gin, straight.

Denise showed McLean and Fried in. As usual they were spatting. Denise got them both drinks and played hostess.

Hardy could hear Holmes barking petulantly in the bedroom as he answered the door. Thorpe and Friday had arrived at the same time. He greeted them both and brought them into the living room. He had to talk to the policeman, but as he did, he peevishly watched Thorpe going over to Denise and kissing her hello.

The characters were all there, now to set the stage. It was simple. Hardy just kept the booze flowing.

Finally Price said, "All right, we're here. And I admit I'm enjoying myself . . . but truthfully . . . why?"

"Ah, my good man," said Hardy doing a bad W. C. Fields, "I thought you'd never ask. Point of information, the young Spanish lad they have downtown has only today admitted that he did not kill Kate Arnheim. If you do not believe me, ask my friend Mr. Friday, who happens to be a minion of the law."

Friday nodded. "It's true."

Hardy continued, but without the fake voice, "That means Kate's murderer is still out in the world, among us."

Henry Pritchett ventured, "But if the boy didn't do it, why did he say he did?"

"I don't know," Hardy admitted. "To get more attention, I guess, or a lot of other reasons peculiar to his own psychology. . . . Who knows?"

Fried and McLean were both pretty drunk. Fried tried to tug his friend back down to the couch, but McLean persisted and stood up to say his piece. "Simple. That fellow Norse did it." He plopped right back down again.

At that point the doorbell rang. While Friday went to the door, Hardy used the interim to fill all the glasses and listen to the confused gabble.

Friday was back. He showed Hardy the package in his hand and set it on the tilt-top table.

Hardy smiled, but only to himself. Then he took the center of the room, pausing only long enough to take the package in his hand. "I have a theory. The killer's own clothes got very bloody when poor Kate was killed, so the killer took one of Kate's dresses, and using it as a disguise, left after the 'dreadful deed was done.'" Hardy was a little drunk himself. "But the killer must have been in the building all the time, before and after the deed."

151

He looked around the room at each one of his guests. Then he started to undo the package. "James Norse told me an interesting thing the day he died, but I was too worried about my skin to pay much attention to him." Now Hardy was unfolding the brown paper. "He said, 'I gave her money and a lot of nice clothes. You should have seen the last dress I got her, a pretty blue one with white on the collar.'" Hardy stopped talking and showed the dress. McLean made a gurgling noise.

The private detective kept his patter going. "I should have remembered that dress. I had seen it. Not in Kate's apartment. Norse gave it to her the day before she died. I hadn't seen her for more than a week before that. But I had seen the dress. Hadn't I?" And he turned and looked toward the couch.

"Don't be an ass," said Ronald Fried. "You're such a fool with all the games you play. Nobody's impressed with the roles you play."

Fried was quite drunk and quite angry. "Patrick Hardy, stud, and Patrick Hardy, detective, we are not amused. You are a big flop. Obviously the police have been to my apartment . . . if they didn't have a warrant, I am going to sue. So they got the dress from my closet. I admit it. I also admit to wearing it on occasion . . . actually it looks very good on me. . . . Well, why not? It was a present from a dear friend who is now dead. . . . Ted, take me home."

And they were gone.

Patrick Hardy scratched his head and wondered how his big confrontation scene had gone wrong. Nothing had come out the way he had planned.

The other guests stayed for a few uncomfortable minutes and slowly they left too. Hardy looked first at

Denise and then at Friday, trying to think of something to say.

Denise started to clean up and then stopped. She sat on the couch and said, "I'm sorry, I must be dense, did I miss something?"

"No", Hardy answered, "I did . . . the boat. Honey, go on home. I'll call you."

"But . . ."

"But me no buts . . . please."

Hardy listened as the front door closed behind her and as Holmes, still in the bedroom, barked his annoyance. Hardy lit a cigarette.

Friday finished his drink and picked up the dress. "Not like the paperbacks is it, Private Detective?"

"No", said Hardy, "I guess it isn't. Come on, I'll walk you outside, I need some air. Are you going to have a hard time explaining why you needed a warrant to get that dress?"

"I guess so," said Friday. "Forget about it. Teach me to stop listening to private detectives with crazy ideas."

Hardy thought about going in to get Holmes but decided against it. Outside the two men walked uptown to where Friday had parked his car.

Just as they passed the corner Hardy heard a sound.

"Gerry."

"Right." Friday had heard it, too, and by this time both could see it. Ted McLean had Ronald Fried up against a wall and was punching and kicking and doing everything to inflict pain.

"You bastard, you lousy bastard," McLean yelled as he kept pounding away. "You fooled them but you can't fool me. You did kill her, but you made it with her first, didn't you? You went to bed with that tramp. How could you do it to me?"

Fried was crying. "Stop, Ted. I love you, only you."

Friday made a move toward the two homosexuals.

Hardy put a hand on the cop's arm. "Wait, Gerry," he whispered, "let them play the scene out."

Friday shook him off. "Sure and have some good citizen complain about how a policeman stood by while one man beat up another." Contrary to his words Friday stayed where he was.

"Stand up, you bastard", said McLean, "I'm going to tell you about the lovers I've had. I'm going to make you suffer the way I did. Remember David in Boston. Well David and . . . Stand up, you bitch, I'm talking to you." And he hit him again. "Before David there was Joe and . . . and before Joe there was Tommy and . . ."

Suddenly Fried lashed out with a right-hand slap. McLean staggered back. "Enough", shouted Fried.

"No," McLean shouted louder, "then there was Arnie and Phil and . . ."

"But they were all fags," Fried answered, "and you're a fag. A goddamned fruity fag. I'm not a fag. I made it with Kate. . . . and Kate has made it with all the studs in New York. I'm not a fag, I'm a stud."

Hysterical, he fell into McLean's arms. "I'm not a fag. I'm not a fag."

"Ronny baby, if you forgive me I'll forgive you."

"Shut up, you fag," said Fried to his friend. Then he ran a few feet and stumbled into Hardy and whispered, "He's a fag . . . I'm not a fag. Ask Kate, she'll tell you. Kate made a man out of me." And he started to cry. "I didn't mean to kill her, honest to God I didn't, but she shouldn't have laughed at me when I couldn't do it."

Friday shook his head in disbelief. He took the "Miranda" card out of his pocket and said, "Mr. Fried, before you say anything else I have to advise you of your rights." He then proceeded to tell Ronald Fried about self-incrimination and that he didn't have to say a word until he spoke to a lawyer.

"I don't want a lawyer. I want you to arrest me and punish me. I killed Kate. I didn't mean it, but it happened. Arrest me. Punish me." Fried was sobbing uncontrollably.

Ted McLean stood there mute, staring vacantly at Friday and Hardy.

"I'll be a sonofabitch," said Friday, and he shook his head at Patrick Hardy. "No fuss, no mess, no bother. Killers just walk right up to you and confess, just like in the paperbacks. I'll be a son of a bitch."

Chapter Seventeen

It was the next day and Hardy and Friday were back at the Chinese restaurant. They had finished eating and were smoking cigarettes. "You were wrong about the dress," said Friday. "He didn't use it as a disguise. It was to walk on so he wouldn't get blood on the floor. Fried had a problem a lot of gay people have, he wanted to be straight, and he figured Kate Arnheim was the one who could do it for him. When he was sure McLean was asleep, he put on his raincoat and shoes . . . nothing else. . . . and sneaked down to her apartment."

Hardy cleared his throat and put out his cigarette, but said nothing. Friday went on.

"When he told Kate what was on his mind, she said why not, but when he couldn't function, she laughed at him. He grabbed the letter opener from the night table and stabbed her. Here's the sick part, stabbing her turned him on. While he was hacking her up, he made it." Friday shuddered, "I've been a cop a long time, but this guy gives me the creeps."

Hardy nodded and called Henry over and ordered two drinks while Friday went on.

"He was actually proud of it. Said it proved he was a man because he had an erection and an orgasm with a woman. When it was over he wiped the blood off with her robe. Then he used his raincoat to step to her closet and took her dresses out and used them to make a path to the bathroom. He told us he read lots of stories about blood traces being found in the tub or the sink where the killer had washed himself, so he washed himself off in the toilet bowl . . . Jesus Christ, the toilet bowl.

"Then he poured cleanser into the bowl to make sure it was clean. The way he told it, you would have thought he was giving helpful hints for the housewife on a TV show. He covered his hands and feet with plastic food bags and put the bloody clothes in a big plastic garbage bag and went back to his apartment where he cleaned himself up and hid the bag, then he woke McLean up and pretended he had been there all the time. Later when he was able, he washed all the clothes in bleach and cut them into little rags. . . . He's been throwing them away bit by bit all this time."

Henry was back at the table again, this time with dessert and the check. Hardy put down his drink and reached into his pocket.

"Keep your money, Private Detective. This one's on me. I've been doing all the talking, now it's your turn. Usually, I can't get you to shut up. . . . Talk."

"About what?" said Hardy.

"Stop breaking my chops," said Friday. "We both know that if you hadn't come up with the dress angle, Fried might never have fallen apart the way he did—

thanks to McLean. But what I want to know is, what made you suspect him in the first place?"

"Just the dress, Gerry, just the dress."

"There was more to it. What else?"

"Haven't you ever read Sherlock Holmes?"

The policeman made a face. "Yeah. When I was a kid."

"Well, just recently I reread "The Beryl Coronet" and in it Holmes answered Watson when he asked a similar question."

"Balls."

"Don't interrupt," said Hardy with a grin on his face. "I don't think I can give you the exact quote, but he explained that when he discarded the impossible, whatever was left, no matter how improbable, had to be the right answer."

"And Fried being a fag, no matter how improbable it was for him to rape a woman, had to be it?"

"Elementary, my dear Friday."

"Crap, with that logic, it could have been McLean."

"I never thought of that," said Hardy, digging into his ice cream. "Since they were in and out of each other's apartments so often, he could have put the dress there . . . but he didn't, so my logic must be right."

"Bullshit," said Friday. "Some detective."

Watch for

Hung Up to Die
A Patrick Hardy Mystery

Visit

www.speakingvolumes.us

Visit us at www.speakingvolumes.us

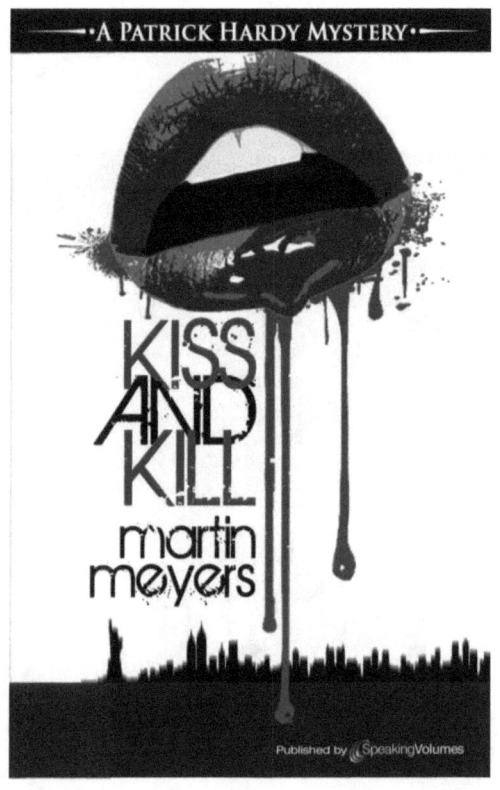

Visit us at www.speakingvolumes.us

**FIND OUT WHY
THE CRITICS LOVE THE
HISTORICAL MYSTERIES OF
MAAN MEYERS**

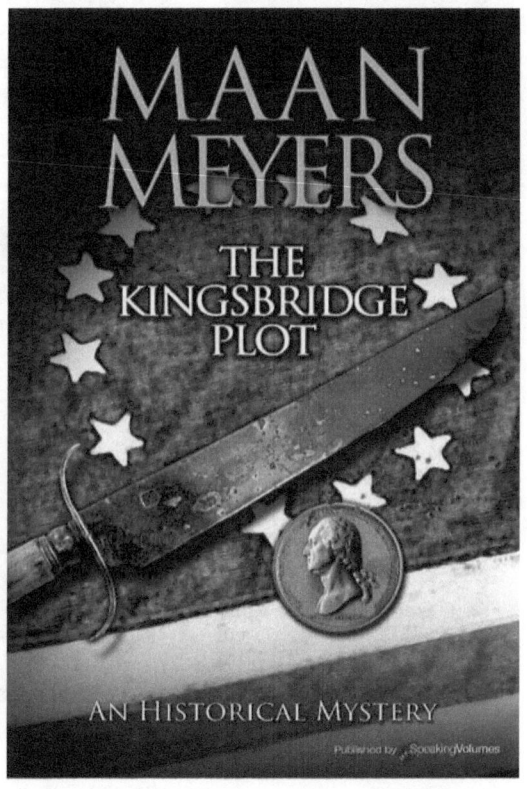

Visit us at www.speakingvolumes.us